PORTRAITS

Of Flowers

and

Shadows

READ THE OTHER TITLE IN THE
PORTRAITS SERIES!

AVAILABLE NOW!

PORTRAITS

Of Flowers
and
Shadows

ANNA KIRWAN

SCHOLASTIC INC.
New York Toronto London Auckland Sydney
Mexico City New Delhi Hong Kong Buenos Aires

For my mother, Catherine Lunsford Kirwan —
six kids under twelve, and she still made time
to read us Little Women;
and for my brothers, Dave and Jim Kirwan —
I watched how they drew and learned how to see.

ISBN 0-439-71010-3

12 11 10 9 8 7 6 5 4 3 2 1   5 6 7 8 9 10/0

Printed in the U.S.A.
First printing, October 2005

All boats are small on the great sea. The ship flew up and fell so, it was like being tossed on a blanket. Mama would not take Aurelia up on deck. The little room bumped up and down. It smelled of boots and fish and lamps, and it was loud, creaking like a hundred giant rocking chairs. Back home, Uncle used to bundle her in her quilt and rock her, and she'd look up at his dear, scarred face until he dissolved into her dreams.

"Is it bedtime?" Aurelia asked. It was dark, and she felt plumb worn-out, and thought Mama must be, too. But then there was a great, crashing thump, and Aurelia fell right off her bunk. The big bell started clanging, and the sailor with the tattoo of Old Abe the Eagle came and knocked on the door and said, "To the boats, ma'am!" Everything was so loud, Aurelia was frightened. Mama wrapped the whole comforter around her and pulled a big oilcloth cloak around herself. She lifted Aurelia and carried her as if she were still a baby, not five years old, and the sailor brought the little blue trunk with red-and-silver good-luck flowers painted on it.

Captain was up on deck. It was raining hard and cold, and the noise was not like rockers up here — it was like giants howling. Aurelia knew it was the wind in the shrouds.

All boats are small on the great sea, and Captain did not get into the little boat with Mama and Aurelia. The sailor did, and another sailor as well. Captain watched, saying, "God bless and save us all," as they were lowered away, and then, "We shall meet ashore in good time!"

When the little boat hit a big wave that came up and walloped them from underneath, the sailor with the tattoo said, "Norman's Woe, b'God, and this here time of year, God help us." They slid down between walls of water so heavy and dark, Aurelia couldn't help but hold her breath. Mama unclasped her cloak and put it around Aurelia and her quilt, so they wouldn't get any more soaked. One sailor took up a bucket and threw water overboard, while the other pulled the oars. Aurelia held on to Mama's drenched woolen gown with one hand and a loop of rope with the other. She did not know what the rope was tied to, but she expected at any moment to be blown right out of the boat.

The sailor who was bailing shouted like the preacher. "The waters swirled about me, the abyss enveloped me; seaweed clung about my head. Down I went . . . but You brought up my life from the pit . . . my prayer reached You . . . source of mercy. . . ."

Mama pulled Aurelia close, and Aurelia could feel her trembling, like one of Grandma's hens when you cuddled it against your pinafore and stroked its warm, soft feathers. Mama's hair was soaked. She looked like a seal under the blue lightning. Her voice was strong and warm, though she didn't shout quite so loud as the sailor.

"They were filling and were in peril," she said. Aurelia didn't know

who "they" were, but she listened to her mama without interrupting. "So they came and woke him, saying, 'Master, we are perishing.' Then He arose and rebuked the wind and the raging of the water, and they ceased, and there came a calm. . . ."

Then Mama sang for a while, and Aurelia fell asleep.

Chapter 1

BOSTON, MASSACHUSETTS

APRIL 1870–JUNE 1878

"Now, Aurelia, dear," Mrs. Sinclair asked, "Mrs. Prentice explained to you about my eyewash and my gargle, did she not?"

"Yes, ma'am, she showed me just how you must have them," Aurelia reassured her. She did not bother to remind the lace-capped old lady that Mrs. Prentice had not been her housekeeper for three months.

"Of course." Mrs. Sinclair picked at a loose thread she imagined on her black cashmere sleeve. She made a sour face. "I'm afraid my nerves are so delicate, I'm forgetful. E. Hancock says I'd forget my own head. . . ."

He says everything that is mean, Aurelia thought — though she did not wish to say so to his aunt. Instead, she plumped the plush cushions on the sofa and patted it invitingly.

"Shall I bring you a pot of tea before I make your bed?" Aurelia suggested, although the routine so rarely varied, she scarcely needed to ask.

"Yes. The silver pot. You know Paul Revere made my teapot? *The* Paul Revere?"

"Yes, ma'am. You told me."

"Did I? I'm afraid I forgot. E. Hancock says I'd forget my head if I didn't tie it on with my cap."

"It's a lovely cap," Aurelia said, patting the cushions again, draping a shawl around Mrs. Sinclair's shoulders as she settled her on the sofa.

"And you're a lovely little girl," Mrs. Sinclair said, her eyes bright as a bird's. "A splendid example for everyone to see. Charity is its own ornament."

"Yes, Mrs. Sinclair. You're very kind to me. Thank you, ma'am. I shall get the tea."

By the time she brought the tea tray five minutes later, with the silver service and the Wedgwood cup and saucer, Mrs. Sinclair's mood had shifted.

"Where's my spoon? Is that the only one you took from the sideboard? E. Hancock says I forget to count the spoons. Look at this sleeve, it's all unraveled — Mrs. Prentice didn't teach you proper sewing."

"Do you want to change your gown so I can mend it?"

"Certainly not. E. Hancock is coming to dinner. I'm ready for morning tea, now."

"Shall I put the sugar in for you?"

"Certainly not! She's a lovely little girl. A splendid charity . . ." Mrs. Sinclair's voice trailed off. She waited for Aurelia to put the sugar in: one lump, two . . . three. . . .

All aboard the windjammer bark *Aspiration* had been lost, wrecked on the notorious reef called Norman's Woe — all, except for one. Mr. Sanborn, a librarian, went out to Milk Island three days later, to see the earliest birds returning from winter, and found a lifeboat bobbing near the tideline. In it was a hungry little girl with black curls, alive in the embrace of her drowned mother.

A lovely little girl, the Gloucester Sailors' Family Aid Circle appealed to Mrs. Sinclair, a wealthy Boston patroness of their society. *No one has claimed her. Her whole family must have been lost but, as no minor was included on the passenger list, she has no last name. We named her for the gentleman who discovered her, Mr. William Sanborn. Due to a clerical error, she was entered into the town records as Aurelia Sandborn. . . .*

Aurelia remembered being brought into the parlor in her fancy, new black silk frock; she remembered curtsying before all the callers. They would urge her to have a seedcake, a bon-bon, a peppermint. Mr. E. Hancock Sinclair, the nephew who lived with Mrs. Sinclair, always had horrid, sharp-edged sucking candies that tasted like cigars, and he always insisted she have one, as if it were a great pleasure, and watched to make sure she didn't wastefully spit it out into her handkerchief. Mrs. Sinclair's friends would fuss over her until the housekeeper, Mrs. Prentice, took Aurelia away. Mrs. Prentice always knew when the little girl had had enough seedcakes and enough of Mr. E. Hancock's pocket-linty candies.

Mrs. Prentice taught Aurelia to read, once she realized the shipwrecked child knew her ABC's already. As Aurelia had grown older, Mrs. Prentice began bringing her to the ladies' tea talks, the public library, the Universarian Transcendental Literary, and the Family Aid Circle, where Aurelia was introduced to Mr. Emerson and Mr. Alcott, and Miss Louisa Alcott read the group a charming story from her book *Aunt Jo's Scrapbag*.

Mrs. Sinclair had taken Aurelia in and paid her upkeep, but Mrs. Prentice kept up Aurelia's dearest hope, that Aurelia's family was looking for her and would trace her someday. The Family Aid had supplied the information that Captain Daniel Shank's *Aspiration* was out of Philadelphia.

Aurelia couldn't actually remember her family, except for her mama — she thought she remembered her mother. There were two pictures in her locket, a photograph of a man and an ivory of an old-fashioned lady, but she didn't know who they were. Aurelia couldn't remember thinking of her father as a real person. He might have been the handsome man in the locket, but Aurelia found only confusion in her heart when she looked at the pictures.

"Your father obviously went down with the ship," Mr. E. Hancock liked to say, "as my own did. Except mine was in the South Seas — probably eaten by the cannibals. A hero's death. Yours just sank with the bark. Right there, off Gloucester. Eaten by the codfish, I daresay. Pity." He had said that yesterday. He had paused to poke a finger into his ear, rub vigorously, extract it, and examine its tip. "Don't expect him to come to the door. Unless he's one of Mrs. P.'s spirits with seaweed in his vest pocket, and all that." He'd been making fun of Mrs. Prentice, since she'd retired and gone away.

All of Aurelia's problems had begun when Mrs. Prentice left; all of her *new* problems, at any rate.

Back in February, Mrs. Prentice's daughter was living in Concord, and she'd been due to have her first child. So Mrs. Prentice had gone to help out, since she'd done midwifing as well as nursing and housekeeping. She'd taken Aurelia along, because Aurelia was sensible and useful and — being about thirteen by this time — knew a thing or two, including how to tidy up. (Curiously enough, Aurelia always called it "redding up," and Mrs. Prentice's son-in-law, who had traveled some, told her they said that in Pennsylvania. Mrs. Prentice had said, "Yes, I told you, the boat was from Philadelphia.")

Then, a month later, the son-in-law had taken a position in Rhode Island, and Mrs. Prentice had gone off with her daughter and the baby to the big, new house, promising to write to Aurelia when she had a moment or two.

Mr. E. Hancock had hired the first applicant to answer his advertisement. Mrs. Blanchefleur had offered him a sample of her white bread, which, with a bit of butter, had quickly finished the interview to their mutual satisfaction. Mr. E. Hancock had hired her on the spot to be housekeeper.

Mrs. Blanchefleur, however, was a very large woman with very tiny feet that were understandably in a perennial state of violent protest. Not only would she not do upstairs work (and this included cleaning upstairs chamber pots), she could scarcely manage to climb the stairs at all. All of the bedchamber cleaning thus fell to Aurelia. Since Mrs. Prentice had left, she was no longer Mrs. Sinclair's protégée. Nowadays, she was just "the upstairs girl."

In fact, beyond the kitchen, Mrs. Blanchefleur's housekeeping consisted mostly of seeing that the laundry got done every week, and that Aurelia gave Mr. E. Hancock anything he asked for — hotter shaving water, extra towels, a snifter or a toddy, or an extra scuttle of coal for his grate toward midnight.

It was not a part of her work that Aurelia liked to dwell on, the part that had to do with Mr. E. Hancock. There was something about him lately that just . . . well, there was something about him. Maybe he did not know how to talk to her without Mrs. Prentice's helpful presence: Goodness knew, he was awkward of speech as well as of movement.

"Are you aware?" he would muse in his wisest tone — and then produce some ridiculous geographical bit of information, such as, "In Japan, the emperor has bathhouses full of servant women, just to scrub his back." But lately he would say even more embarrassing things, which Aurelia did not know how to answer.

Last night, for instance, when she'd brought him his coals, he'd spoken to her from where he stood leaning on his armchair, sipping his second toddy.

"Dark down there in the cellar, isn't it?" he remarked. "Now, are you scared of a dark corner, Aurelia?"

"No, sir," she answered.

He sniggered as if she'd said something improper. "No, *you* wouldn't be scared. I guess *you've* seen everything, now, hey? That was a manchild you saw delivered from his mother, wasn't it? Yes, I expect you know all there is to know about some things, don't you, miss?"

When Aurelia had ignored his remark and attempted to whisk away downstairs, he had stepped so suddenly into the doorway that she could not get past without his brushing against her. She hated how he always did that lately. A grown man, forty years old at least, acting that way! He was almost like a rude boy at the market, when no grown-up was looking. Almost, but somehow, worse.

When Aurelia was finished with Mrs. Sinclair's tea, she hung up the flannel nightdress and tucked the lace-trimmed nightcap under Mrs. Sinclair's pillow. *She used to remember to be kind,* Mrs. Prentice had said regretfully, *poor old thing. Just to think — losing track day by day. . . .*

After putting Mrs. Sinclair's things in order, Aurelia went up the back stairs to her own room on the top floor and made her own bed. Then she fetched water, and was stealing a moment to rinse out her stockings, when she realized she was not alone.

"Now, that reminds me," Mr. E. Hancock said in his whiny voice, "you *might* come down to my closet and see to *my* boots and stockings. I'm invited to a reception."

"When is it, sir?" Aurelia asked. She had to recover her composure after the abruptness of his appearance. What was he doing on the third floor, anyway?

"Tonight. Don't you wish you were going?" he said, stepping nearer to her. "It will be an elegant gathering, I assure you, with dancing, and good wine punch. I could bring you back a little, if you like, Aurelia. Would you?"

Aurelia dried her hands on her apron, leaving her stockings in the basin of soapsuds. She turned her back toward her narrow bed and her flowered blue trunk — had she left it sitting open like that? She didn't like Mr. E. Hancock following her to her room, but she was not sure how to say so without making him angry.

"Mrs. Prentice would not commend me to it, I expect," she said after a moment. Suddenly, he reached over and clamped a big, tobacco-stained hand around her wrist as if it were a billiard cue.

"Wine punch. And oysters. You'd like that fine, I think, wouldn't you? A fresh little bit of a thing like you? Stay up and wait for me. I won't be out late."

With her other hand, Aurelia scooped her stockings,

dripping, from the basin, and deftly escaped his grasp by swinging them, still dripping, across his sleeve.

"I have to go to Mrs. Sinclair now," she said as he recoiled, and she fled.

"Don't forget about my boots!" Mr. E. Hancock called peevishly after her.

So it had come to this, Aurelia realized. Mr. E. Hancock had never treated her so coarsely when Mrs. Prentice had a weather eye on things. Aurelia knew without a word passing that Mrs. Blanchefleur would not speak up for her to Mr. E. Hancock — not even if he took it into his fool head to order her to scrub his back like a Japanese gentleman.

Aurelia would have to leave. She could not bear to think what he'd be like after the reception, what he had in mind. She would have to depart the Sinclairs' house, where she'd lived since she could remember; and for that matter, the whole neighborhood, where Mr. E. Hancock dined with so many gentlemen that he would surely discover her. Or he could in any event talk about her behind her back, which could be just as unpleasant and dangerous to her future safety. She would have to leave Boston and go to another town.

She would go to the Family Aid Circle, to see if they could recommend her for a position . . . but, no: Mr. E. Hancock would know to inquire for her there.

Perhaps, she thought, she could go to Providence. She

would have to ask Mrs. Sinclair for some pocket money. She would have to get a letter of good character from her, to show to a prospective employer. Mrs. Sinclair could never write such a letter; Aurelia knew, the minute she thought of it. She would have to write it herself and ask Mrs. Sinclair to sign it.

Aurelia went back into the drawing room, to the writing desk, and took out a creamy page with Mrs. Sinclair's monogram embossed at its head. She was not sure what she ought to say, but she had to write something quickly.

> *Aurelia Sandborn has been with my family for eight years. She is good at needlework and linens. She reads and writes well and bakes good gingerbread. She is good at polishing bureaus, bedposts, wardrobes, and so on with beeswax, and filling and trimming lamps and building fires that don't smoke awfully much. She does not steal nor lie nor drink rum, brandy, nor other spirits.*

Was that all she needed to say to get the sort of job she could manage?

She is good at taking care of chickens and dogs, she added. She was not sure why it seemed the thing to do. The Sinclairs had never kept either a henhouse or a dog, but Aurelia thought she was sure to be good at such work, and might as well try to find it, while she was at it. *And has had some work helping care for a baby.*

"Will you sign this letter of character for me, ma'am? I am going to go to Providence, I believe."

"A holiday? Going on a holiday?" Mrs. Sinclair asked

cheerfully, an expression of genuine interest coloring her papery cheeks for the first time in weeks.

"Going away, ma'am. I need to go somewhere different. To work." If Aurelia thought Mrs. Sinclair would not understand what was happening, she guessed wrong.

"But you're my girl! Who will bring me my tea? Who will sing for me on Sundays when it's too hot to go to church?"

"Mrs. Blanchefleur will engage someone," Aurelia said, feeling a stab of guilt.

"No, no, she's not as good as Prentice, you know. Prentice always gave me baked beans on Saturday, with molasses. Prentice gave me cherry pie every Tuesday."

"I know, ma'am. But I need to go away. I'm too old to stay with you now."

"Nonsense. You're a lovely little girl. What will E. Hancock say?"

"He'll say Mrs. Blanchefleur will engage someone."

"Oh. Oh, yes." Carefully, Mrs. Sinclair wrote her name, *Mercy Starbuck Sinclair,* and admired the effect. "There. Have you a postage stamp to send it? Take some pocket money from my purse, dear. Take five dollars. No, take ten dollars. Get yourself some nice gloves, if you're going on a holiday. There might be dancing, you know. Such a dear little thing. You always did carry on about the chickens."

Aurelia suddenly felt broken inside.

"Thank you, ma'am. Thank you. You have been very kind to me. I won't forget."

Aurelia backed out of the room. She did not wish to linger until Mr. E. Hancock sought her out.

But it was he who was lingering, in the upstairs hall. As she went back up to her room, he suddenly stepped out of a storage closet — and waved her locket under her nose. Mama's locket, which had been in the blue chest. Aurelia knew he thought she would do as he liked, as long as he had it. "If you don't come see me, you saucy thing," he said, "I'll come find you. Someone will have to have that wine punch!"

She did not dare try to seize the locket, lest he discover the letter of character she held hidden behind her back. Then, as he passed her, he made a show of patting her cheek. She looked into his face for one instant and saw there that this was no clumsy, mistaken move on his part, nor even some awkward affection. She shuddered, and a dark glint kindled in his eyes. She could see that he knew he was frightening her, and that he liked thinking she was afraid of him. And now he had her most treasured possession.

Aurelia put her little blue wooden trunk, with her initials — her locket's initials — *A. S.*, inscribed inside the lid, into an unbleached cotton rice sack. She carried this over her shoulder. It wasn't very heavy — all it held was her nightdress, her Sunday frock, her other drawers and good stockings, and her little Bible. She toted it outside, and then downtown, to the workroom occupied by the Daughters of Martha. They didn't help orphans, like Family Aid; they helped working women and the missions. Mr. E. Hancock did not patronize their cause, so far as Aurelia knew.

Aurelia had never had to plan ahead, except when she was sewing or cooking. It was something of a relief to push her feelings out of her mind and concentrate on orderly thinking. She reckoned if the placement service could find her work in Providence, that employer could telegraph funds for her to make the journey. It was only noon — she might be there by nightfall. She wished again that she had Mrs. Prentice's street address. Even if Mrs. Prentice's daughter did not need a maid, someone she knew might.

But then it occurred to her that Mr. E. Hancock would look for her first of all with Mrs. Prentice. She could not go to Providence yet. Not until she was sure he was not looking for her. She wanted never to think of him again. She did not think she could ever, ever explain to anyone — not even Mrs. Prentice — the humiliating reason she had left poor Mrs. Sinclair so abruptly, with no one to bring dinner to the old woman.

Chapter 2

Almost a year later, Aurelia still had the sense that Mr. E. Hancock should never get wind of her, and that she had to keep an eye out for him. To be on the safe side, she had even written to Mrs. Prentice using "General Delivery, Townsend" instead of her new address.

In Townsend, she hadn't told anyone about her past. She knew the story of the shipwrecked child was a memorable oddity, and a rumor could too easily make her whereabouts known. But she had learned, to her surprise, that no one asked more than one or two questions about her family or background prior to her last place. Depending on how they phrased their inquiries, she could often give a vague reply about Boston ways, or "It's a long time since I talked to them."

Her new employer, Albertine Ellicott, did not pry. She had enough to do.

Amity, the daughter, scorned to inquire. She was sure it should not interest her.

Aurelia had only been in Mrs. Farwell's class at the high school since January, so she and her teacher were hardly acquainted yet. At school, everyone knew she was Amity Ellicott's housemaid, and she was not particularly sought out at lunchtime. Usually Aurelia sat quietly, overhearing other people's chatter, and, depending on her mood, trying not to listen, or trying to figure out whom they were discussing and to learn names.

Last June, when she had desperately applied to the Boston Daughters of Martha, to know if anyone outside of Boston was looking for an upstairs girl or kitchen help, the secretary told her there was a position in Townsend, the town that made the barrels the Daughters filled to send to the missionaries in tropic climes.

Mr. Ellicott, the gentleman who wanted domestic help, owned a sawmill. The family was well heeled, Aurelia was given to understand, although nowhere near as well-to-do as the Sinclairs. Their big house was not in the country, it was in one of the better neighborhoods; but, then, Townsend was not an especially elegant town.

"No chickens," the lady at the Daughters of Martha had admitted. "But they do say there is a rather irritable parrot. They will only pay eight dollars a month, but you will have your room and board, and will be allowed a term at the high school each year, due to your age." Since the Sinclairs had not sent her to public school or paid her any sort of regular wages at all, it had sounded luxurious to Aurelia.

The village of West Townsend was up the road from Townsend Center. It was not out in the country, but it was not what Aurelia was used to. Main Street in front of the Ellicotts' house was not paved, though there were stately houses up and down the block. The Ellicotts, in fact, had never had a serving maid before, for Mrs. Ellicott was a brisk, efficient woman who enjoyed cooking, gardening, and all sorts of useful labor. But their mill was prospering, and they were glad to give up unnecessary frugality. Sixteen-year-old Amity had so many demands on her time, so many invitations and shopping excursions with her friends, her parents had feared her health might suffer, so they had applied to the Daughters of Martha to find them some good help.

And even though the "room" provided had turned out to be an unheated sleeping porch where Aurelia froze all winter, and the parrot not merely irritable but ancient, ugly, and cruel, and the household contained not only the endlessly social Miss Amity, but also the mostly irresponsible son, twelve-year-old Union — Aurelia did not think she was badly off — for the most part.

The first time Aurelia was introduced to Miss Amity, she stood silent, waiting for the stylish young lady to speak first.

"I am pleased to meet you," Miss Amity said. "Union's the one who needs the most cleaning up after — he's a little pig. Don't touch anything on my dressing table, don't come into my room without washing your hands first, and don't try polishing or dusting any of the furniture in my room. I really don't like scratches."

And I don't, either, Aurelia had thought, vowing to give Miss Amity as wide a berth as she possibly could.

The chief thing was, Mr. E. Hancock would never think to look for her in Townsend. Probably never. It was almost a year, already — he couldn't *still* be trying to find her. Why would he? He had stolen the only thing she owned that was worth anything — her locket. And even a real family stopped looking for you after a while.

The work at the Ellicotts' was not awfully hard, though there was lots of it. Besides the family and the evil parrot, Cicero, there was also a dog that thought he was Aurelia's. To be precise: Union had a gray terrier for which she inevitably had become responsible, which had spent all winter on the sleeping porch with her. The dog's name was Uncle Adams. Aurelia had just now secured him within the screened portion of the porch, because he was not supposed to follow her to town, but would, if he could.

"May I go to the library, ma'am?" Aurelia asked her employer nervously, aware it was the third time within a week she had applied for the privilege. "Miss Amity is in the kitchen, watching Miss Elima crimp Miss Livia's hair." *And making the place smell like a fire at the livery stable,* she added to herself.

Mrs. Ellicott paused on the front stair. "But we must suffer for beauty," she said with a shrug, gazing bemused at the odd housemaid the Daughters of Martha had furnished her with last summer. After almost a year, the girl remained a puzzle. Aurelia had quietly fitted herself into the household work and the neighborhood's normal life, but it was still rather a mystery where she had really come from. Mrs. Worthy, at Townsend's chapter of the Daughters, had assured the Ellicotts that Aurelia Sandborn came recommended. She was an orphan, gently reared and educated, not afraid of hard work or domesticated birds. Yet she had this unnerving habit of speaking to her employers, however courteously, as if her opinions were as pertinent as theirs.

"Yes, ma'am," Aurelia replied calmly, refraining from tossing her own glossy black tresses, which needed no curling iron. "But the teacher assigned me to memorize a piece that is close to being the longest poem in the world." She tried at least to make her complaint in a sympathetic, reasonable tone of voice. "You see, I have to say this poem in front of everyone for Decoration Day, which is in a few weeks — and, beg your pardon, ma'am, but the smell of Livia's burnt offerings jars my mood when I am trying to concentrate."

Mrs. Ellicott shook her head and wrinkled her nose. "Did you bring in the sheets off the clothesline?"

"Yes, ma'am, and I hung out the tea towels and stockings and Sunday shirts."

"And did you clean out Cicero's cage?"

"Yes, ma'am." *And almost lost my thumb to his vicious beak.*

"Well, I suppose you may go, then. I expect it's better to do your assignment before you set the table. Please remember to give my regards to Miss Calantha."

"I'll remember." Mrs. Ellicott must know the librarian from church, Aurelia thought. She certainly never took out books, herself. Neither did Amity.

Mrs. Prentice couldn't have gotten on without the library.

Aurelia checked her bonnet in the hall pier glass, caught up her library books, and hurried out the door. Just as her mind was settling into the beginning lines of her recitation piece — *By the flow of the inland river / Whence the fleets of iron have fled* — her attention was captured by the sight of Mrs. Mattie Homer, the Ellicotts' neighbor across the street.

Mrs. Mattie in maroon serge bloomers, riding a high-wheeled bicycle uphill along Main, toward Canal. Mrs. Mattie was actually riding her bicycle. Union reckoned she'd never do it. But Union was, after all, twelve: He purely scorned all persons not that same, perfect, age.

Mrs. Mattie — Aurelia had watched her from across the street with considerable curiosity. Mrs. Mattie could do anything she put her mind to, Aurelia reckoned. Then she went back to her silent reciting.

> *Under the sod and the dew,*
> *Waiting the judgment-day;*

Under the laurel, the Blue,
Under the willow, the Gray.

Aurelia turned the other way, toward Townsend Center. The May sunlight was so warm, the violets in front of the house were already fading. It was a twenty-minute walk to the library.

Wayland Harrigan might be there already.

She had met Wayland last July, when she'd just come to Townsend and hadn't started her term at the high school yet. His family lived in the North Village, over on Nissiquassick Hill. But Mr. and Mrs. Homer always invited all the local students to their Independence Day picnic and gave every youth in town a shiny twenty-five-cent piece for firecrackers. Wayland was seventeen back then, soon to start his senior year. Who would have thought he'd speak to her?

It was actually quite magical, Aurelia thought, how they had become acquainted. They had both been standing near the counter at Howe's, waiting to purchase their share of squibs, torpedoes, and Roman candles. Mr. Howe, who knew everyone, had introduced Wayland to Aurelia casually, saying, "Miss Aurelia, now, she has plenty to do, yonder at the Ellicotts.'"

Later, over on the lawn at the Homers', Wayland had actually come up to her, offered a cup of lemonade, and asked courteously if she were related to the Alcotts of Concord. By the time she had explained that he'd misheard the name, and anyway it was her employers', and although she was not really an Ellicott *or* an Alcott, she was honored to be associated with one of her favorite authors, whom she once, happily, had met. . . . Wayland had asked insightful questions, and a genuine conversation had begun. It was a conversation that had continued, now and again, through the ensuing year — a conversation mostly about books, but sometimes . . . *branching out,* Aurelia liked to think.

She crossed to the left side of the street so she wouldn't have to walk past the establishment of Miletus Gleason, Undertaker. Aurelia recalled the voice of Mr. Gleason, who was on the School Committee and the Sniffing Committee, which enforced the blue laws, and who was afflicted with an unfortunate speech impediment. At the school's Lincoln Memorial Assembly last month, in April, Mr. Gleason had read the very poem she now labored over, "The Blue and the Gray," by Francis Miles Finch. *"By the fwoe of the inwand wiver/ Whence the fweets of iwon have fwed . . ."* he had read with great feeling.

Gweat feewing, Aurelia had heard herself thinking.

And Mr. Gleason was the reason Aurelia had to memorize the same poem, and recite it in front of practically the whole town. While Mr. Gleason had read, Aurelia had smiled to herself, and her teacher, a war widow, had raised her eyebrows almost up into her cap and effectively extinguished

Aurelia's tactless amusement. Then, directly after the assembly, she had assigned Aurelia the Decoration Day recitation.

During the War Between the States, Mrs. Farwell's husband was shot in the neck at Cedar Creek. Their only baby died of rheumatic fever that same year. Mrs. Farwell still wore only black dresses.

> *No more shall the war cry sever,*
> *Or the winding rivers be red;*
> *They banish our anger forever*
> *When they laurel the graves of our dead!*

Aurelia didn't remember anyone who'd died in the war. She probably hadn't even been born until 1865, when the war was almost over. Fourteen years was a lifetime ago.

Before she came to Fussburton's cooperage yards and railroad siding, where the road crossed the Squannicook River, she paused and balanced her books against the bridge railing. There had been snow upcountry so late in April, the river was still high, noisy, and black-glass cold with the runoff of New Hampshire's melting. She had a stitch in her side from walking rapidly. She tried to breathe from deep under her rib cage, as if she were in singing class.

Bloomers like Mrs. Mattie's would make walking a lot easier, Aurelia thought. A little while later, she was carrying her armful of books upstairs, past the shirts, collars, and cuffs counter at

Flagg's haberdashery. The public library was situated in the upstairs rooms. It was hard not to trip, climbing the stairs without being able to hold one's skirts. She tried to hold her books low enough so she could clutch her skirt up, just a little, at the same time. She did not cut a graceful figure, but neither did she tumble down the stairs, so she counted the plan a moderate success.

Wayland was there. He had slung himself into a black leather armchair under a window. The light fell right across him — chair, book, and all — his russet hair, his corduroys, his boots up on the carpet-upholstered ottoman.

It was always a pleasant shock to behold Wayland. He persisted in being even more handsome in person than Aurelia dared paint him in her mind. She did not see him every day at the high school, because of their being in different classes. He was across the room from her now, but she could take in his whole grace of form, the careless ease of posture that betrayed his absorption in the green book he held in his right hand. He leaned on his left elbow, cheek propped against his fist. The west window highlighted his tousled hair and his forearm to the wrist, where the cuff had come unbuttoned.

He had not noticed she had walked in, she thought. She felt herself flush. It was embarrassing, not to be noticed at all. It was somehow even more embarrassing than being noticed. It left everything up to her.

"Are the girls in Boston all such mooncalves?" Amity twitted her last week. "Say you *are* fourteen. He is *graduating* this June. Don't dare to embarrass me! You must act your age and not have ideas about young men already shaving."

"I don't believe he shaves very often," Aurelia had protested stoutly. "Besides, he is reading all of the works of Ralph Waldo Emerson."

"What that has to do with it, I can't see."

"What shaving has to do with it, I don't see," Aurelia had retorted. "I have been introduced to Mr. Emerson, so, naturally, I am also going to read all of his works." *Not that Amity would understand!* Actually, Aurelia thought she would take her time reading *all* of Emerson. His thoughts were exceptionally high-minded, and a person had to be in the mood. But Miss Amity need not act as though she were better than anyone.

Aurelia could see that Wayland had shaved his chin recently. He had a small nick, unbandaged — like a thorn scratch. But nothing so boring as a thorn scratch, she was sure.

Aurelia had meant to take her returned books to the librarian Miss Calantha Crofoot, first of all. That was what she usually did when she came in. But she had taken a step toward Wayland almost without noticing.

He looked up.

There were rock doves nesting on the ledge outside the window beyond him. Aurelia could hear them cooing and squabbling out there.

"What's new?" she whispered.

"*Against Fate*, the new novel by Mrs. Rayne," Wayland whispered back. "Terrible stuff, by the look of it."

"You mustn't judge a book by its cover." Aurelia suppressed a smile at the melodramatic face he'd pulled.

"One chapter is called 'Judas in Petticoats,'" he informed her disgustedly. "I read a bit of it, before thinking I could be more usefully occupied."

"I'm sure it's good for some," Aurelia suggested doubtfully, but Wayland shook his head and rolled his eyes in droll impatience.

"Mrs. Rayne seems not so good a soul as your Aunt Jo," he whispered decidedly.

"Aunt Jo" — meaning Louisa May Alcott — was a joke between them.

Amity didn't understand: They had jokes between them.

"Then, what are you reading?" she asked.

He waved the green book toward her, and she had to take several steps to approach close enough to read it: *The Adventures of Tom Sawyer* by Mark Twain.

"Not brand-new, but it's a go-bang."

"Not Emerson?" Aurelia asked timidly.

"Oh, well. Taking a break from Mr. Waldo's essays. I

have them at home. I read three pages a night — that's plenty to think over."

Miss Calantha cleared her throat. Aurelia was facing her — she looked up from Wayland to see the librarian beckoning her with one index finger as she shushed them with the other.

Miss Calantha sent greetings back to Mrs. Ellicott and asked Aurelia to take a book to Mr. Charles Homer, Mrs. Mattie's husband. It was a science book, about shellac insects. Mr. Charles was a chemist — he'd invented a special varnish for railroad cars. One coat was as good as seventeen coats of old-fashioned varnish. Insects in the shellac or varnish would be a problem, Aurelia saw that. However — a whole book on the subject? Mr. Charles's business must be exhausting. But she did not mind carrying it with her own books. It was handy sized and would scarcely add anything to the burden of her own choices, whatever size they were.

Wayland was still sitting, reading, she saw by a quick sideways glance. She wondered if he had already checked out his books with Miss Calantha, if he would disappear before she could choose her week's batch, and see if he found them interesting. She went to the book table rather than the index card catalog. If she sent Miss Calantha off among the bookshelves looking for a book, she would have to wait for her to come back and check it out. She would not be able to catch up with Wayland, and they would have no pleasant farewell moment like the one last week, with his brown eyes teasing her when he said, *"Go to your lessons, now, Not-Really-a-Alcott."*

She selected a gold-stamped blue novel from the recently returned volumes: *Uarda*, by an Egyptologist, Georg Ebers. It had no illustrations, but was well supplied with footnotes. Aurelia thought Wayland would probably not call it "terrible stuff," though it seemed rather dense to be a real go-bang. She also took Edward Lear's *Nonsense Songs, Stories, Botany, and Alphabets*, and an issue of *St. Nicholas Magazine*, with one of Mrs. Hale's funny stories about the Peterkin family. Sometimes the amusing drawings gave you just the lift you wanted, taking you right out of the words and making you feel you were there.

"Now, you will be sure to take Mr. Charles's book over to Mrs. Mattie directly, won't you?" Miss Calantha fretted. "It has just arrived, and he requested it weeks ago."

"Even before I go back to Ellicotts,'" Aurelia promised. She wondered if Mrs. Mattie would still be wobbling about on the high-wheeler.

Wayland was turned, watching her over his right shoulder as she walked toward the stairwell — which was to say, more or less toward him.

"You're going to the Homers' house?" She nodded. "Train's not until five-ten."

"I'm walking."

"My Da is over there, working for Mrs. Mattie. We're supposed to go over to the fire company meeting in the West Village this evening. I'll walk with you, if you like. Are you game?"

She was game.

Chapter 3

The nesting birds were twittering by the Squannicook, and the wild cherry buds were blowing open in a haze of tiny white petals.

As they walked, Wayland told her a little about Mammoth Cave, and Tom, and Huckleberry, and Injun Joe. A little, but not enough to give the whole story away. He said she'd like it, though.

They also talked about Graduation, which was to occur on the Sunday after Decoration Day. Wayland was not the valedictorian, an honor earned by poor Cornelius Miles, who had a clubfoot and could not run about but instead sat and studied, day in and day out. However, Wayland was ranked third in the senior class and thought he might take the prize for Latin.

Aurelia finally worked up the courage to ask a question that had been much on her mind. "Will you be leaving for Cambridge in the fall?" Wayland had told her that his first goal in life was to study at Harvard, where he could hear Emerson, himself, lecture.

Wayland's handsome chin tipped up a shade more decidedly. He looked thoughtful. "Well, perhaps not this fall. Haven't got the spondulix saved up yet. I have *some* of the money — I ought to! Been working since I was eleven."

"How much does it cost to go to Harvard?"

Wayland shook his head ruefully.

"Four hundred sixty dollars a year, tuition, room, and board. I've got about half that much saved."

Aurelia thought of the little slide-top wooden salt-cod box where she kept her savings. At present, they totaled $10.17. She had earned eighty dollars since she had been in West Townsend, but she had spent most of it. She had needed winter clothes, and though she'd made some of them herself, using patterns she'd traced from *Frank Leslie's Lady's Magazine*, the yard goods hadn't been cheap.

Most of her March pay had gone for a new dress for Decoration Day. Last summer's Sunday frock was pink sprigged lawn, too childish and merry for her somber recitation. And, Aurelia was sure, too tight in the bodice, now, anyway. She was making herself a slate-blue organdy over sky-blue chambray, with simple lines and a tucked bodice, French lace sleeves, pale yellow collar and cuffs, and smart little square buttons.

"Miss Calantha went to Bridgewater Normal so that she could teach at the Female Seminary," Aurelia said. Before the war, the seminary had been an elegant school for girls, right there in West Townsend. "Sometimes I think I'd like that but . . ."

"But . . . what?" Wayland asked.

"I don't know if I'll want to keep going to school every morning *forever*," Aurelia confessed. "I have discovered that half a year of classes suits me well enough. I like books pretty much always, but I only like school compared with . . . I don't know . . . shoveling snow?"

Wayland laughed.

"You're a funny little thing," he said.

Aurelia reddened. She felt her heart thrill at the fond expression on his face as he said the words.

But she was not so sure she liked the words. She was up to his shoulder already, and still growing.

"I'm not so little," she said.

"'*The microscope cannot find the animalcule which is less perfect for being little,*'" he said. "Mr. Emerson says." He was grinning.

"As long as you acknowledge me perfect," she said haughtily, "I shall overlook the 'animalcule' remark."

"Actually," Wayland offered in a conciliatory tone, "you aren't little — just stooped over from all those books you're toting. What a beast I am, not carrying them for you." Graciously, he reached over and took her armful, and added them to his own.

That was before they'd reached Haseltine's Music Store. As they wended their way past, Aurelia caught a glimpse through the gilt-lettered window. Livia Twitchell's family had a parlor organ, and Livia was in Haseltine's, poring over the newest sheet music selections. Miss Amity and another friend, Elima Worthy, were with her.

Aurelia wondered if any of the three fashionable misses had happened to see Wayland Harrigan walking with her, carrying her books. Who would have thought he'd carry a mooncalf's books?

When they strolled up to the Homers' front gate, they could hear voices from the drive out by the stables. One was Mrs. Mattie's, and another, it turned out, was Wayland's father. Gerald Harrigan was standing with Mrs. Mattie's two grooms, Mr. Thomas Roebuck, who was English, and Mr. Alphonse Peabodeau, who was not, and with Mr. Charles Homer. They were all standing around Mrs. Mattie's high-wheeled bicycle.

"'Ere it is," said Roebuck. "Yer've got a pebble in the pivot."

"I can have that out straightaway," Mr. Harrigan said.

"That is the only problem I encountered, keeping it balanced," Mrs. Mattie declared. "Charles, it is a splendid machine! You are the kindest of husbands!"

"Bayliss-Thomas," Mr. Harrigan informed Wayland. He worked a shift at Fussburton's, but he was also Mrs. Mattie's bicycle mechanic. "Light as a feather."

"British," Mr. Roebuck pointed out.

"We'll see how it holds up compared with a good old American Harvard cycle," Mr. Peabodeau remarked mildly. He had what Mrs. Sinclair used to call a South Boston inflection. Mrs. Prentice had told Aurelia that meant Irish.

Mr. Charles and Mr. Harrigan leaned the tall bicycle against a granite hitching post, and Mrs. Mattie dismounted. Aurelia thought Mrs. Mattie must be close to Mrs. Ellicott's age, but the loss of her only infant, years before, had left her to fill her days with friends and various healthful hobbies.

"Hello, dear," Mrs. Mattie said to Aurelia directly. "You've brought Charles his bug book — good girl. Charlie, Miss Calantha sent Aurelia with your book!"

Mr. Charles was crouching in the driveway with Wayland's father, the grooms, and Union. Union had apparently put himself in charge of Mr. Harrigan's toolbox and was handing things to him on command, for the privilege of watching the bicycle repair up close. Aurelia just knew Union was going to be asking his own father for a bicycle, next thing. Mrs. Ellicott had already stated that she thought he was still too small to manage one safely.

Wayland grinned at Aurelia, and she noticed that she'd hastily gathered one of his own books from his arms, *A Wreath of Shamrocks* by John Keegan Casey. It appeared to be a book of poetry.

Wayland's teeth were fine and white and almost even, and his grin was a little lopsided but not much. His eyes were deep and lively. Even when he was entirely still, and his gaze steady, Aurelia could see ideas moving like lights in Wayland's eyes.

A boy named Laurence Boutelle came around the house from the front walk. Aurelia only knew his name — he was one of Amity's set. Slightly out of breath, he had a telegram in his hand. He handed it to Mrs. Mattie.

"Charlie, here's a telegram from Winslow!"

"Blast," said Mr. Charles. "I've axle grease on my hands. What's he say?"

"He — oh, my!" Mrs. Mattie read aloud: 'ARRIVING WEST TOWNSEND TUESDAY STOP SORRY FOR SHORT NOTICE STOP AFRAID CLARE SKYE IS LOST STOP YOURS AFFECTIONATELY WIN.' *Today* is Tuesday! Who is Clare Skye?"

Mr. Charles stood up, unthinkingly wiping his hands on a linen handkerchief.

"His favorite sailboat. Toy schooner. When we were boys. The day after Father left for California in '49, Win took her out to the beach to sail her, instead of to the pond. He thought he could manage her, but the tide was running, and she got beyond him and . . . I don't remember if she smashed up, or foundered, or what happened, exactly."

For a moment, Aurelia felt bleak.

"Whatever does he mean, then, by '*Clare Skye is lost*'?" Mrs. Mattie puzzled.

"My poor brother has had something unfortunate happen and is coming to you, Mattie, to have his sorrows mended. As we all do."

[34]

"But — my reception and dinner are this Saturday! We have one hundred guests coming for the reception at the Elmwood House, then twelve for late dinner back here! Another house guest — and your father due in, as well!"

"Oh, Winslow won't want in on the party," Mr. Charles said soothingly.

"I have to do all the floral adornments, too," Mrs. Mattie fretted on. "I need seven conservatory bouquets for the tables and piano. And I need garlands of greenery. Mountain laurel. Ropes of it. Oh, how am I going to get it all done? You're going to be off, fishing with your brother . . . Aurelia!"

Mrs. Mattie's eye had fallen on her neighbor's hired help.

"Aurelia, dear. Would you like to help me with my dinner for Mr. Fussburton? You know how to tie up laurel into garlands, don't you? There's all the mountain laurel we need up by the Ash Swamp, I'm sure. You did it at Christmas with evergreens, didn't you? Yes, you did, I remember — Albertine's parlor was splendid! How would you and Union like to earn some spending money?"

Spending money, Aurelia thought. *Spondulix.*

"I don't know if Union will help," Aurelia considered, "but I will do what I can."

"I shall be glad to help," Wayland said politely to Mrs. Mattie. "My father works for Mr. Fussburton. Is this dinner to honor his running for Congress next year?"

"Yes, it is, and I do want the party here to be just as fine a party as in Boston, and better! The laurel is just about to bloom, and it will look absolutely elegant. Laurel for victory! If you children will bring me as many yards of laurel roping as you can manage, I shall pay you well for your time and trouble!"

Aurelia could scarcely believe what had just happened.

"Shall I meet you here after school tomorrow?" Wayland said to her. "Can you bring some sacking, or some baskets, to carry the branches? It will take lots of trips, but with you and me and Union, we can do it."

"Oh, yes," Aurelia managed to say. "There's a big thicket of laurel up above the canal near Mr. Ellicott's mill. We can start there."

"We'll be partners," Wayland said. "Sandborn and Harrigan."

"Sandborn, Harrigan, and Ellicott," Union said over his shoulder from where he was sitting in the driveway. "I'm saving up for a Bayliss-Thomas."

"We can share whatever we earn," Aurelia agreed. She admired how self-reliant Wayland was, working for his goals in life. She wondered if it was fate that she could help him meet the great Mr. Ralph Waldo Emerson.

And she knew she would see him tomorrow.

Chapter 4

Aurelia was met at the front porch door by the moplike Uncle Adams.

"*Huh-woh,*" the terrier prompted as Aurelia set down her books and untied her bonnet. It was the amusing creature's trick to "speak" thus to anyone arriving who did not, straight off, pat him in greeting. Mr. Ellicott said Uncle Adams made a better host than guard dog.

"Hullo," Aurelia answered him, hanging her hat up, and finally giving the impatient pup his much-desired pat.

The house no longer smelled of Livia's burned locks; it was now filled with the aroma of roast lamb, rosemary, and thyme. With Uncle Adams doing his best to walk betwixt her ankles like a cat, Aurelia shook out the clean, blue-checked everyday tablecloth across the big oak dining room table. Everyone's napkins were in their napkin rings — Mr. Ellicott had whittled them, and each was unique. His own was marked with an acorn, and Mrs. Ellicott's with a maple leaf. The children's had designs reflecting Mr. Ellicott's pet names for them: Amity's, a kitten showing its mittens, and Union's, a handsome globe onion with a fine braid of leaves.

Aurelia wished she had one, too; a napkin ring, or a pet name, either one. But then, she supposed a person simply had to have a family to have some things. Mr. Ellicott liked his family dinners to be private, so Aurelia ate in the kitchen and read, interrupted by the bell when anyone in the dining room wanted seconds, or a spill mopped up.

In the kitchen, Mrs. Ellicott was basting the leg of lamb. A bowl of tiny early peas stood on the pine table, next to the jug of cream that was to be poured over them when they were steamed tender.

"Here you are," Mrs. Ellicott hailed Aurelia, "just in time to see to the rhubarb sauce. Mr. Ellicott has to have supper early this evening. The fire volunteers are meeting tonight."

"What does the rhubarb need done?" Aurelia asked.

"It's already cut up and soaked — just drain the water, throw in a couple of handfuls of sugar and a *soupçon* of cinnamon, and when I take the lamb out, put the rhubarb into the oven. Without slamming the door — there are popovers in the side oven."

Carefully pushing the roasting pan back in for its final browning, Mrs. Ellicott demonstrated her warning by closing the oven with a gentle click.

"How is Miss Calantha?" she asked, turning away from the hot work and smoothing wisps of her hair back from her flushed face and tucking them under her cap.

"Looking well. We didn't talk much — other people were reading." *Wayland was reading.* "She gave me a book to bring to Mrs. Mattie." *And Wayland walked me all the way home.*

"And how is Mrs. Mattie?"

"She has a bicycle, and she was wearing bloomers to ride it, and it looks so easy! Mrs. Ellicott, I believe I would like to make myself bloomers."

"You will not! The idea! You are an unmarried girl! Mr. Ellicott would never hear of it while you are working here, I am sure."

As this was, more or less, the reaction Aurelia had expected, she said nothing.

"If you are ready to fit the waist of your new dress," her employer said by way of peace offering, "after dinner, come up to the sewing room, and I will pin it in place."

"Mrs. Ellicott, bloomers are more modest than skirts that can blow around."

"Aurelia, it is what people would *think.*"

Perhaps I don't mind what people think, Aurelia reflected. *Why care for the opinion of strangers, if it's always going to be the same old thing they've been thinking since Noah wrung out his stockings?*

Amity and her friends bustled in from the front porch, chattering and laughing. Earlier, Aurelia had wished one of them might witness her pleasant camaraderie with Wayland. Now, though, she found herself hoping they would retire to the parlor without paying her any mind.

"Oh, fie, what a nuisance!" Livia whined. "This dog is the trial of my existence!"

"Aurelia," Amity called sternly, "can't you do something with Uncle Adams? He's about breaking our necks, getting underfoot."

"Say hello and tell him to sit still. If you please, miss," Aurelia told her, for what must surely have been the hundredth time. "He knows how to be a gentleman."

"Like a *certain person?*" Elima remarked archly. "We saw you, you know."

"I should hope I haven't gone invisible," Aurelia said under her breath. She knew she was in for it now.

"Perhaps you'd do better if you *could*," Amity chided. "You'd look less a child, if you'd think before walking next to a person so much taller than you. The effect was comical." Amity avoided looking Aurelia in the eye as she voiced her criticism.

"If you are referring to Wayland Harrigan," Aurelia replied, laying a fork at Mrs. Ellicott's place, then one at Union's, "he did not seem to think discussing geology with me was especially ridiculous." She said it airily. Amity was not at all interested in geology and could give no effective retort.

It was Elima, however, who commented.

"He's quite good-looking, I must say — Amity, are you certain you are not getting tired of Fred Wagner's attentions?

Perhaps you ought to put Mr. Harrigan on your dance card!" she simpered. It was one thing Aurelia disliked about Elima: She was a simperer.

Aurelia began on the knives, going clockwise around the table. It had occurred to her that she had better head off Union when he came home, and warn him not to say anything around Amity and this lot about the laurel expedition.

"'Good-looking'?" Livia was saying distastefully. "Aurelia, my girl, you really would be smart to find yourself some worthwhile beau with connections in Boston. Where you worked before, didn't you meet any suitable people? This Mr. Harrigan — well, he's one of those North Villagers. It's not a good idea to cultivate such an acquaintance."

"I am sure I don't know what you mean, Miss Livia," Aurelia said, thinking it wasn't any of Livia Twitchell's business whom she chose as a friend.

"Well, I'm only saying what everyone says. It's not wholesome, the way they live," Livia explained as if to one who was feeble-witted. "They say it's like a rabbit warren over there. None of them is clean, and they keep pigs in their dooryards."

"Wayland is going to go to Harvard," Aurelia said. "No pigs *there*."

That ought to make her hold her tongue, Aurelia thought. Livia frequently boasted that her father had earned a diploma from that august institution.

"They drink strong spirits," Livia sniffed. "They're super-stitious. I don't know about how it was where you came from, but my father says the Jesuits —"

"Not many of *them* at Harvard, either," Aurelia said. She wasn't quite sure what a Jesuit was — something Irish, she supposed, the way Livia was talking. The Twitchells were not broad-minded about the Irish, the Italians, the Poles, or the emancipated.

"They can just about tolerate the Methodists," Mr. Ellicott had once remarked. "If they are behaving in a sub-dued manner."

And don't have a dog, Aurelia thought.

Uncle Adams had gone into the front hall again and was sitting expectantly gazing at the doorknob. Aurelia glanced out the window and saw Union coming up the walk, rolling a hoop slowly by hand. Aurelia guessed he was thinking of wheels with spokes.

She peered cautiously at the hallway. Amity and the others had only gone into the parlor, not upstairs. Aurelia had to keep Union out of the parlor until she could secure his discretion. Setting down the silverware, she slipped out the French doors onto the big wraparound porch. Union was coming up the steps, hoop hanging over his shoulder.

"Union!" she called softly, before his hand was on the knob. "A minute, please?"

"What do you want?" he asked, not particularly courteously.

"A vow of silence," Aurelia whispered. Now it was spring, all the windows had been opened to air out the house. It was difficult to know if they'd be overheard.

"What did you do?" Union asked pragmatically.

"Nothing. But don't tell your sister about . . . you know."

"About . . . why not?" He was not sounding uncooperative, only curious.

"*Shhh!*" she said firmly. "Back me up, *please*. Those girls are being fools about something or other. Don't let on about Mrs. Mattie and the laurel, all right?"

Union considered.

"You mean, you'd rather do it without them. Fortunately for you, I think you are right, there. Say, how much do you think she will pay?"

"What do we think is fair?" Aurelia shrugged. "We shall see."

"I'll keep quiet on one condition," Union bargained. "Hook me a cup of milk. Ma isn't letting me near the kitchen while she's baking this week."

"You did make her cake fall," Aurelia said, sighing.

"Tasted fine to me," Union twirled his hoop languidly on the wide-plank floor of the porch. "Milk, and I'm mum."

"Let's shake on it," Aurelia agreed. They crooked little fingers to seal the pact.

*   *   *

"May I take Union a mug of milk?" Aurelia asked Mrs. Ellicott.

"Certainly. He is starting his summer growing spell already, and milk is the best thing for the boy."

"Do you think I am starting a summer growing spell?" Aurelia asked.

"I expect you are," Mrs. Ellicott said. "You should run tucks around the hem of your dress — then you can let it out two or three times as you grow taller."

Aurelia poured a tin mug full and carried the milk to her coconspirator.

"Should I ask Pa for my bicycle before he sees Mrs. Mattie, or after?"

"After, probably. Especially if she is going to make a track."

"A Bayliss-Thomas can go a quarter of a mile in forty-seven and three-quarter seconds," Union was saying dreamily when she went back inside. "So, to go to the Center would take . . ."

Aurelia had just brought the covered dish of steaming rhubarb as far as the butler's pantry when Mr. Ellicott got home. She heard the depot express wagon out front and went to the door to look. He had jumped down from the wagon, which was pulled up over by the Homers' sidewalk, and was helping another passenger to unload his baggage: a steamer trunk, two strapped leather satchels, various bundles that sorted out into a collapsed portable artist's easel, a folded-up camp stool, a canvas quiver of fishing rods, and a banjo.

The mustached gentleman to whom Mr. Ellicott and the express man were handing these things was wearing a light tweed suit and a flat, straw boater hat. Aurelia guessed it was Mr. Charles's brother, Mr. Winslow Homer. Mr. Winslow was a real artist, who made pictures for *Harper's Weekly* magazine. He did not look as if he'd been in a shipwreck.

"Mrs. Ellicott, Mr. Ellicott is older than you, isn't he?" Aurelia asked later, after supper, when Mr. Ellicott had left for the fire volunteers' meeting.

"Yes, six years older."

"Do you know Mr. Harrigan, who works for Mrs. Mattie? He's in the North Village fire company."

Her employer looked up from her task, transferring the roast from its platter to a glass dish that would fit into the ice chest.

"I know who he is. Mr. Ellicott knows him."

"Does Mr. Ellicott know his son, Wayland? He's also a volunteer."

"Probably he does, then. Why?"

"He walked me home from the library." Aurelia spooned the last servings of rhubarb into a china bowl and covered it with a saucer. "That was all right, wasn't it? He's a very polite boy, third in his class. And he's saving up to go to Harvard."

"Polite and ambitious," Mrs. Ellicott said thoughtfully. "And brave and dutiful, to join the fire company. And he walked you all the way home from the Center?"

"He had to meet his father at the Homers', for the meeting tonight. He asked if I'd like him to, right in front of Miss Calantha. I thought you wouldn't mind, so I said yes. Did I do right? We had a very interesting conversation, walking."

"Oh, you did? What did you discuss?"

"Books, mostly. And the Boston Red Caps — nine games so far this season, and we've only lost two," Aurelia told her, unconsciously quoting Wayland. "You don't have any objection to my walking with him, do you, Mrs. Ellicott?"

"Oh, I think it was all right this time."

"He's going to help Union and me get laurel for Mrs. Mattie's reception on Saturday."

"He sounds like a very nice young man," Mrs. Ellicott said gently.

"Mrs. Ellicott? He's Irish."

"Harrigan," the good lady said with a laugh. "I did not think he was Algonquin." Mrs. Ellicott's maiden name was Devereaux: Her family had come from Quebec.

"You don't mind?"

"No — how silly! Nor should you! He is an American. He is like us. Now, *allez-y!* Go get the last of the dishes, and come wash them up. I shall ask Mr. Ellicott if he knows Mr. Harrigan's polite son."

Remembering to fetch Union's tin mug, undoubtedly abandoned when empty, Aurelia stepped out onto the porch.

Twilight had turned the village blue. It was beautiful. It could have been under the sea, Aurelia thought. Even the brilliant colors of Mrs. Mattie's tulips had muted to gray and buff, and the first stars shone among the treetops. The whole street was still. It would have been silent, as well, except that someone was playing a banjo. Aurelia's eyes swept across to the Homers' place.

There he was. Mr. Winslow was sitting alone in the shadows on the front steps. He was playing an old soldiers' song, "Tenting Tonight."

Aurelia had never heard a banjo sound so forlorn.

Chapter 5

Aurelia walked home from school trying to think of all the places in the woods nearby where she knew there was laurel, and deciding which of the kitchen baskets would be best suited for the task. Except for the laundry baskets, she reckoned, none were big enough. They would have to make many, many trips into the woods and back, to have enough greens to garland the whole dining room in graceful swags.

When she got home, though, and had changed out of her blue-and-yellow calico into the sturdier myrtle-and-bronze merino that had been her everyday dress last fall (but would never fit her by next September), she was chagrined to realize that the laundry baskets were filled, as she might have guessed, with laundry.

Union was sitting in the Hitchcock rocker in the kitchen, eating an oatmeal snap and drawing a spidery high-wheeler on a piece of brown paper. Aurelia paused to observe the drawing. The cyclist's cap bore the initials of Union Sterling Ellicott. Two droll little men stood to the side admiring the sight. A ribbon issuing from the lips of one of them showed that he was saying, *He will be there in 382 seconds!* His companion rejoined on his own ribbon, *By Jove, we are saved then!*

"Onion, where's the Nantucket basket?"

"Ma used it to bring the rhubarb in from the garden yesterday," he said. Aurelia went into the box room at the back of the kitchen and, sure enough, there was the lidded basket with the red stripe around it. Next to it was the wood-slat gardening basket, heavier, but sturdier; safer to entrust to Union. Finding nothing else that would do, she went back to the kitchen and put all the folded laundry from one of the big baskets atop the still unfolded pile in the other one, hoping Mrs. Ellicott would not mind, just for the afternoon.

Then she tied on the garden sunbonnet she wore for working outdoors. It was old-fashioned white muslin, and Aurelia thought it made a person look like theater posters of Lotta Crabtree; but it was what Mrs. Ellicott had given her to wear, and it was what other Townsend girls wore when they weren't going into town. So Aurelia tucked away her best feature (so she thought), her gleaming locks.

"Ready?" she said anxiously. "We ought to go before Miss Amity gets in."

"*That* slow boat," Union scoffed. "She'll be waiting at Howe's Store, eating all her nickel's worth of candy before she leaves the place. She says it's because you shouldn't eat on a public street, but she just doesn't want to share."

"She just doesn't want to walk away from Fred Wagner any too soon, you mean," Aurelia corrected him. "He's working for Mr. Howe after school now."

"Want to know!" Union approved. "See if I don't turn that to some benefit! That ought to be worth a few spearmint gumdrops if I'm persistent."

"Not now!" Aurelia protested. "We have to see if Wayland is at the Homers' yet."

"Oh, I don't mean now," Union agreed airily. "I'm just thinking about my future."

Aurelia had not anticipated the donkey cart, but there it was in Mrs. Mattie's drive. The miniature steed wore a raffish palm-leaf field hat and an expression so alert it might have been elfin. Wayland stood chatting with Mr. Peabodeau.

"Hurrah!" cried Union. "Just like the ones at the seashore!" The animal's ears swiveled.

Aurelia had a fleeting thought of Amity, Livia, and Elima. She imagined their expressions should they happen to see her sitting on the narrow seat with Wayland driving, while Union rode in the wagon, *and* the expressions they would show if she rode in back with Union. She was not sure one vision was any worse than the other. And so she hoped, if ride they must, to ride up front with Wayland and watch his hands on the reins. Wayland was always writing reams of essays; his fingers were inevitably spattered with faded and fresh ink. With his red-gold freckles and his black and silver-gray ink blots, Aurelia liked to think of him as dappled.

"Here's how we use our time to best advantage!" Wayland hailed them. "Uncle Michael is going to bring this big tarpaulin up to Mr. Ellicott's mill yard for us, and then come back with old Corker in an hour or so to pick up whatever we've gathered by that time. You brought us each a basket — capital! They can go up the road in the cart, too."

He and Union, between them, produced five different pocketknives, all recently whetted, one of which (it just happened to be Wayland's) Aurelia borrowed.

"Union," Wayland marshaled him, "if you'd like to ride — you and Uncle Michael will both fit." It seemed Mr. Peabodeau was the uncle to whom Wayland referred.

"How long after she ordered it did it take" — Union was asking Mr. Peabodeau now — "for Mrs. Mattie's Bayliss-Thomas to be delivered?"

As if offended at the mention of his rival's name, old Corker let out a bray.

"Whoa! Where's the oil can?" Union laughed. "He's a rusty bit of machinery!"

"He's noisy," Wayland acknowledged ruefully. "But he's strong as Atlas, and not bad-tempered, though he is independent-minded!"

"In answer to your question," Mr. Peabodeau said, calmly tidying the beast's forelock, "I believe it was sent for last

March, and has just arrived this week." Union looked stricken.

"If I'm to have any of the season left for riding, we'd best start earning our greenbacks right away!" he urged.

Old Corker cheered the idea.

Aurelia handed Wayland the willow laundry basket. Wayland smiled as he took it from her and put it in the back of the cart.

"May I say, that shade of green is fetching on you, Miss Sandborn."

Aurelia felt herself redden.

"Why, thank you, sir," she said. "That's why I wore it. For fetching laurel."

Union climbed into the back of the little cart. Seated in the straw strewn in it, with the baskets, it was a snug fit. He and Wayland's uncle made cheery jibes at the size of each other's boots and the proper distribution of elbows. Uncle Michael took the driver's seat and flicked the reins.

It was a pleasant amble up the Ashby road to the sawmill, and the cart did not bother to go far ahead of Wayland and Aurelia — only far enough that they were able to converse without Union overhearing every word.

Wayland undertook to explain his uncle's French pseudonym. One of Mrs. Mattie's Boston friends, the story went, had taken the Grand Tour of Europe and, upon returning, had made much to-do about the French driver she had brought back. This had amused Mr. Charles so much that he had immediately dubbed Michael Flanagan "Monsieur Alphonse Peabodeau," telling Mrs. Mattie it would be more economical to offer the local man a bonus for answering to a different name than it would be to pay to import a genuine Frenchman.

Aurelia enjoyed herself immensely, until they reached the mill yard.

They were just strolling up, and Union was clambering out of the cart, when Miss Amity stepped out of the mill office, snapping the clasp of her purse. She was apparently just coming from negotiating with her indulgent papa for a bit of extra shopping money. Lydia Twitchell was waiting for her in a carriage.

Amity pretended she didn't see them. Union made certain she did.

"Look!" he shouted. "We're off to the seashore! We're going sea bathing!"

Old Corker let out a noble whinny, and Aurelia froze.

Amity looked outraged and mortified. Livia began talking directly into her ear, the moment she was in the carriage. The Twitchells' driver was mercifully quick to rouse his grays and take the stylish girls away. Goodness only knew what they were discussing.

"We don't need any big branches," Aurelia told Wayland and Union as she took the borrowed knife out of her pocket and headed purposefully toward the stone canal that had been abandoned since the town's early years.

The laurel grew thick, upridge beyond the pines north of the old mill race. Reddish bark zigzagged at knee level and interlocked under swirls of glossy leaves. Everywhere, the breast-high boscage was starred with clusters of bead-sized pink buds, ribbed like sea urchins. A few flowers had already flung themselves open — the branch tips held them out, alabaster fairy goblets set with rubies. Or so Aurelia thought.

"Just hand-sized little bunches of leaves on twigs," Aurelia explained to the fellows, who had never made up garlands before. "The stems shouldn't be too long, or the garland won't hang gracefully."

"When our baskets are full, we can take them up to the mill yard and empty them in one heap until Uncle Michael returns with the cart," Wayland suggested, "and then come back to the bushes and get more."

Union was staring at the three clusters of greens he had cut and dropped into his basket already.

"If she wants *ropes* of this stuff, we've a lot to do," he realized with dismay.

"Ropes," Wayland confirmed. "Hawsers. Cables and chains of it. She wants the whole dining room rigged." He tucked a rosette of leaves over his left ear, just under the brim of his cap. "Look, I'm Apollo," he said, "crowned on Olympus." He cut one cluster of the white buds, which were just starting to open, and offered them to Aurelia. "I expect you must be a dryad or naiad of some sort."

"I'll be one of the Muses. Thalia," she decided. "She had to do with poems, didn't she?"

"The comedies," Wayland grinned. "Do you write poems as well as read them?" he asked, evidently ready to be impressed.

"I'm still really a green writer," Aurelia admitted. "I can't seem to avoid rhymes that slant like the Tower of Pisa, and my punctuation isn't always what it should be. But I'll get better. Even though every time I go near the sewing room, Mrs. Ellicott has apoplexy if I don't bleach the ink off my fingers before I even thread a needle."

"Let's go, let's *go*," urged Union. "My bicycle will take three months to deliver, even after it's paid for. I want to ride it before I'm as old as *you!*"

Two hours later, they were slogging their way back to the West Village center through the Ash Swamp. They had made trip after trip from the laurel copses to the mill yard, and heaped up the leaflets of laurel a good four feet deep. After an hour, the donkey cart had reappeared, and they'd transferred the harvest into its capacious bed. At that point, they discovered that Old Corker had indulged himself in a nibble on one handle of Mrs. Ellicott's laundry basket.

"Onion," Aurelia moaned — for he was the last to have

toted the basket — "why'd you leave it sitting where he could eat it?"

"Oh, don't carry on, you Boston crybaby," the boy had rudely replied. (It must be noted, everyone was rather hot and tired by this time. Of course, that was no excuse for bad behavior.) "Just go cut some osiers down by the river. Ma can fix that — she and Miss Calantha make those baskets for the church bazaar every couple of years."

So, leaving Uncle Michael the task of bringing the cart back to the Homers', they made their way downstream along Willard's Brook. Where the ground grew oozy, they removed their boots and stockings, and hung them by the laces around their necks, so the heels thumped in front at every lurching hop from dry spot to not quite dry spot.

As they made their way, Wayland quoted a handsome piece of poetry, which he said was by the ancient Roman Horace, about the son of a slave whose father had paid for his education. He said a bit in Latin, and it sounded mysterious and magical; but when he translated it into English, it was more amusing and satirical.

Then Union began his recitation piece from last spring.

"'*It was the schooner Hesperus,*'" he droned, "*that sailed the wintry sea. . . .*'"

"Oh, don't," Aurelia interrupted him abruptly. "Don't make me listen to that!"

"No Longfellow?" Wayland inquired, surprised. "I thought everyone admired 'The Wreck of the Hesperus.'"

"No shipwrecks. No . . . *woe*. Please?"

"Oh, well," said Union, "I don't like the hideous thing, myself. It's just the longest one I ever had to memorize."

"Which is it?" Wayland asked, though. "No shipwrecks? Or no woe?"

"No beautiful, orderly poems about shipwrecks by old men who weren't there, recited by little boys who weren't there," Aurelia said. She thought she sounded crabby. But she really did not want to think about it, let alone talk about it, she told herself. Mr. E. Hancock used to relish quoting Longfellow's verses about a Gloucester shipwreck and a girl who froze to death. It had always made Aurelia feel desperate to get away. "Sorry, Union. I meant, by schoolboys."

"All right," Union said complacently. If it had been Amity, he wouldn't have resigned so easily.

"Have you read the *Odyssey*?" Wayland asked. "I'll bet you, that was by someone who'd been there!"

As they hiked back toward Mrs. Mattie's yard, they had gathered a few last, irresistibly choice clusters of blossom into the lidded basket Aurelia had feared to surrender to the donkey cart. Wayland and Union had just located a clump of young willow wands and were plying their knives smartly, when, from the tangles of sassafras and blueberry no more than fifty yards or so away, they heard a man's voice.

"Here, you rascal, what are you about? Blast! Home, you! Get away! Go back where you belong!" They heard a loud splash, another "Blast! Where are you off to now?" and Uncle Adams, soaked and dripping duckweed, came wriggling out of the bushes — followed after a moment by Mr. Winslow Homer, his trousers, up to the knees, also soaked and dripping duckweed.

Chapter 6

Uncle Adams was all over the lower reaches of Aurelia's skirt with his wet front paws.

"*Huh-woh! Huh-woh!*" he insisted.

"Your hound, is it?" Mr. Charles's brother said to her. Union answered, though.

"Yes, sir. My sister must have let him out. Get down, Uncle! I'll give her what-for, too — see if I don't."

Whether or not Mr. Winslow Homer grasped that Aurelia was not the sister in question was a moot point. He interrupted his own gaze at her sunbonnet to slap at a mayfly behind his ear. His hair was a middle-aged fringe, recently barbered and trimmed short. So, despite his mustache and the straw boater tipped back over his high forehead, the tiny black flies had plenty of skin to beleaguer. Perhaps, Aurelia mused, he was wishing men's hats had curtains around them such as the old-fashioned sunbonnet sported.

"Stand there for a moment, please — don't move," he said to Aurelia in a perfectly pleasant tone of voice. "No, don't look toward me. Take about a half a step backward. Hmm — oh, sorry." He shook his head, and slapped at another insect, but absentmindedly now. "You reminded me of someone. I beg your pardon."

"I'm sorry the dog got you," Aurelia said self-consciously.

"Oh, it was the surprise, not the dousing," Mr. Winslow dismissed her concern graciously. "Not a fellow's best duds he's wearing, out scouting for the wily bass. How's the fishing this year, young man?"

"Mostly pumpkinseeds through this part, near the canals," Wayland estimated, but Union shook his head.

"Took a black bass out last week that was about so big," he informed them, holding his hands about far enough apart to indicate the size of a young porpoise.

"You did not!" Aurelia reproved him, shocked. "It was only about this big. If you had to clean it, you'd think that was big enough!"

"Well, where there's one that size, who knows? He's got an old man somewhere, eh?" Mr. Winslow Homer was gingerly edging toward his left, squinting a little as he changed position in relation to the sun, which stood well above the late afternoon horizon. He was still looking more at Aurelia than not. "Here," he said quietly to Wayland, who happened to be carrying the lidded basket, "would you be so kind as to hand that to the young lady, so I can catch the effect? Look at that — almost a Naples yellow, when it's next to those flowers. Very nice. Very nice. Ought to do some watercolors of them." He might have been talking to himself. "Well. Live around here, do you?"

"Across the street from you," Union told him bluntly. "You're Mr. Charles's little brother, aren't you?" Mr. Winslow looked slightly nonplussed.

"His younger, bachelor brother, I expect you mean," he said rather gruffly. "Everyone knows every consarned thing about a fellow around here. Say, better keep the 'Dog of Flanders,' here, away from the bass, eh? If they're as big as you say, he might be in some danger."

The mustache made it difficult to see if he was smiling or serious.

By the time they got back to Mrs. Mattie's, it was getting on for suppertime. Union and Wayland, together, hauled a big zinc watering trough out of the back of the tool room and filled it about half full of water. They put the greens in the trough in the shade next to the porch, where it would stay cool through part of the day, at least. They'd make the garlands after school tomorrow. *Three days in a row with Wayland!*

Aurelia realized she had better work on her memorizing some more tonight before bedtime, after cleaning up the kitchen and finishing the cuffs for her new blue dress.

> *Under the laurel, the Blue,*
> *Under the willow, the Gray . . .*

"No shipwrecks? Or no woe?" Wayland had asked. About her taste? she wondered. Or about her past?

Aurelia also wondered about the Homers. Mr. Charles's artist brother was shorter than Mr. Charles; about the same age as Mr. E. Hancock, but healthier. Mr. Winslow emanated the same woodsy air and simple elegance Mr. Charles wore, but Mr. Charles had more hair, and his mustache turned down around his mouth at businesslike angles, while Mr. Winslow's turned up like bird wings.

He certainly did look at a person.

Did that feel dangerous? she wondered.

No, Aurelia decided. He was a painter, with a sensible, interesting way of looking.

Miss Amity and the other girls were in the parlor, paging through the latest issue of *Frank Leslie's Lady's Magazine* and evaluating the chic American bonnets and Paris *chapeaux*. Union took it upon himself to enter the parlor and visit the turquoise-and-yellow parrot, Cicero, to ply him with soda crackers and try to get him to say something surprising. (In his earlier years, Cicero had belonged to a sea captain, and he could have put any crew through its drill, once he began to show off his nautical commands.) Lately, this was his favorite way to annoy Amity.

"Say 'Stand off,'" he was coaxing the bird when Aurelia came in to fetch the water pitcher from the mantel. "Say

'Lower the boom!'" He could not persuade Cicero to so much as an *Avast!* though he teased the bird with a cracker he repeatedly poked through the cage bars and withdrew just in time to watch the poor polly reach out with its curious, thick tongue, then pull back, cheated. "Say 'Batten the hatches!'"

"Union," Amity snapped. "You are so aggravating it's no wonder it doesn't care to talk to you."

"At least I don't let him out to fly into the swamp, as you did with Uncle Adams!"

"If you didn't drop a trail of food everywhere you went, he wouldn't be so keen to chase after you," Miss Amity retorted. This was an argument they'd had before.

"If you didn't always flap your parasol at him, he'd come back when you call him back," Union countered.

"You don't suppose a lady can go out on a day like this without a parasol, do you?" Livia chimed in with a disapproving frown. She looked at Aurelia when she said it, Aurelia noticed. Aurelia did not own a parasol.

"You don't suppose a lady can't remember the dog is likely to be inside the screen porch if he's not tied up by the maple tree," Aurelia said, half under her breath. It just slipped out, but Livia and Amity both pounced.

"I had other things on my mind than the dog," Amity protested sharply.

"You can't blame her for being distracted," Livia said silkily, "when she'd just seen a member of her family with the hired help, flouncing around town like a parade of circus animals! Why, if Fred had looked out the shop door just then, Amity, I would have felt so humiliated for you! He's only working at the store to learn business, you know. It's really banking he's to engage in. A young man must protect his prospects from undignified displays, of course, just as a young lady must! A word to the wise!"

"That donkey! Honestly!" Elima flapped her hand on her wrist as if she were shaking out a dust cloth.

"No one was flouncing," Union protested heatedly.

"We were invited to help Mrs. Homer," Aurelia said coolly. "Anyway, in the hills of Tuscany, rustic carts like that are considered picturesque." (Wayland and she had discussed Tuscany that very afternoon.)

"West Townsend is not the hills of Tuscany," Amity said in an acid tone, "and taking care of Union's dog is not *my* job."

"And if you are going to associate with certain sorts of people," Livia said piously, "you must expect to be judged by the company you keep."

"Present company excepted, I assume you mean," Aurelia said as sweetly as her concealed fury allowed. "Miss T*witch*ell."

When Aurelia finally escaped to set the table, she could still hear the girls talking.

"You're only watching out for *her* prospects and morals!"

Livia exclaimed. "The ingrate! She's kitchen help! You must not encourage such impertinence, my dear!"

"Yes — because she's from Boston, or Rhode Island, or Plymouth Rock, or wherever, does she think everyone in the country parades around and makes a spectacle of themselves with farm animals in the middle of Main Street?" Amity said bitterly. Aurelia could practically see her roll her eyes.

"With that boy who goes to the fire meetings with the men," Elima pointed out.

Their voices hushed then, except Amity said the words "No! . . . want to know!" rather too loudly.

Aurelia wondered how they could possibly object to the fire volunteers. Mr. Ellicott was a fire volunteer. Even Mr. Miletus Gleason was a fire volunteer.

The sailor with the tattoo of Old Abe the Eagle had a knife in his hand, and he cut the rope, and one end of it disappeared. The rain stung like the yellowjackets out behind the coop at home. There was blue-green ice on the sailor's strangely long eyelashes. There was feathery white ice on Mama's eyelashes. If she cried, there would be ice on her own eyelashes. They were being driven onto the Galilee shore. When the sea took him, his knife fell as if it were going to cut her and she yelled —

"Look out! Watch it!"

She was sitting up in her iron bed on the second-floor sleeping porch. She had woke up when someone yelled . . . when Uncle Adams barked. . . . They knocked on the door and pushed it open. Mrs. Ellicott, in her nightdress and nightcap, was carrying a kerosene lamp. Mr. Ellicott was right behind her, with his nightshirt tucked into his trousers and, of all things, his malacca Sunday walking stick upraised in his hand.

"What's the matter?"

"What happened?"

"I . . . it was a bad dream," Aurelia realized. She felt horribly sad, so sad that it made her hollow and sick, and a shiver passed through her as she tried to remember what it was about. She pulled the thin wool blanket closer around her. "Something was falling — a tree, or . . . a flagpole, or . . . something. . . . I'm sorry I woke you," she added as she became more awake and her mind cleared. Uncle Adams was on the foot of the bed, not curled up, standing looking at her in the dim lamp light.

"But nothing real?" Mrs. Ellicott was relieved.

"Just a bad dream."

Mr. Ellicott took the kerosene lamp from his wife and went downstairs and all around the porch outside, making sure nothing was amiss.

"Go to sleep," he said, not unkindly, when he came back.

Aurelia did not get back to sleep immediately. She did not want to repeat whatever dream had so frightened her. Mrs. Prentice would have said to light her lamp and read Scripture. Aurelia felt too tired to bother with the lamp, or with finding a bit of Scripture that would speak to her right then. Anyway, were there chapters and verses on how to keep believing your family might someday find you, even if Mr. E. Hancock couldn't? She would never fall asleep if she started worrying about Mr. E. Hancock.

She thought of Wayland reading three pages of Mr. Emerson's essays each night. She was quite certain it would soothe her to do that, but the lamp was still too much trouble. She wondered about Wayland's house, where he was probably sleeping at that very moment. She wondered what he was dreaming. Wayland's mother had died of typhoid fever ten years ago, and so had his little sisters and brother. He had two older brothers, grown men. One was a railroad mechanic out in Chicago, and the other was a priest somewhere in New York State. She wondered if Wayland said his prayers every night, the way Mrs. Prentice thought everyone should.

When Aurelia thought of saying her prayers, she remembered Mr. Sanborn wading out through the lapping blue-gray seawater to lift her up out of the icy, rocking boat, picking her up as if she were a baby in a cradle. She remembered seeing the long scar on the man's cheek when he leaned over her. She thought of that song they sang at the Universarian Transcendental Aid Circle — how did it go? *He shall raise us up on the last day. . . .*

Chapter 7

"Miss Worthy is coming by with her carriage, so we can enjoy the apple blossoms on the way," Amity informed Aurelia. For a fleeting moment, Aurelia thought she was being invited to join the other girls in a leisurely ride to school. That was not Miss Amity's intention, however. "Would you please do a proper job on my room today?" she continued, averting her eyes as she adjusted the panniers at the sides of her skirt. "A few young ladies may stay here overnight when their parents are at the Homers' gala on Saturday, and I don't know when I last saw the floor of my closet!"

Aurelia rolled her eyes. Amity always tried on three dresses every time she selected one, and never rehung any. She also moved her furniture around in her room frequently, leaving everything she had previously shoved under the bed stranded mid-floor like seaweed at the high tide line. Other than changing the bed linens and doing the normal sweeping, Mrs. Ellicott never asked Aurelia to clean up Amity's things. Aurelia suspected, in fact, that it was usually Mrs. Ellicott who smoothed the rumpled sashes and laces and put the pretty frocks away. It was the most baffling thing to Aurelia, of all she had encountered in West Townsend: that a grown-up young lady of Amity's age and fastidious ideas of behavior never appeared to consider that she made extra work for her own mother. Didn't she realize how fortunate she was, even to *have* a mother?

Let alone, a dozen becoming gowns!

But Aurelia was determined that she was *not* going to be redding up Amity's room this afternoon while Wayland was over at Mrs. Mattie's trying to get the laurel garlands made. She would simply have to get the room done before leaving for the Center. And she would have to catch the next train, to arrive at school in time to be marked tardy rather than absent. Mrs. Farwell always made cutting remarks about students who arrived late.

Aurelia sucked on her thumb where she'd scooped up a snarl of hairnets and velvet snoods and stabbed herself on a beaded hatpin.

Paper bonbon wrappers, discarded calling cards, a hairbrush; Miss Amity owned an endless number of things, things, things. Aurelia hung up the sprigged yellow lawn with amber sateen points, and bundled cuffs and collars of three or four different outfits. She almost stepped on a tiny silver mechanical pencil that had been carelessly slipped into some pocket and then dropped.

If I had a pencil like that, Aurelia thought, depositing it in a pin dish on the washstand, *I would spell better than Amity does.*

But she resolutely put aside base envy. She did spell better than Amity, even without the cunning pencil, and such thoughts did not clean up the overturned bandboxes, scorched curl rags, and empty jars of rosemary bandoline hair pomade.

The train pulled in as Aurelia was catching her breath after the run to the depot. She was glad that she'd had only her books to carry and no parasol. But she thought she could have run faster if she'd had on bloomers like Mrs. Mattie's.

"Scholars in other towns may be permitted to be lax," Mrs. Farwell said pointedly as Aurelia slipped into her seat at the back of the classroom, "but here, we stress punctuality. It is essential, if one is not to miss the main chance."

The main chance. Aurelia wondered if she would miss her main chance. She had almost missed the train.

That afternoon, Wayland was not at Mrs. Mattie's when Aurelia arrived, but Union emerged from the toolroom with spools of wire, balls of twine, and a couple of old towels to dry off the soaked laurel. Aurelia looked into the zinc trough. More of the white flowers were open, but nothing was wilting yet. In a few minutes, the two were both seated comfortably in the shade on the grass below the side porch of the house, each with the first cubit or so of twine already wrapped in evergreen.

When Wayland arrived a few moments later, his coming was heralded by a clatter of pebbles and metallic rattling, as well as joyous barking — not only from Uncle Adams, tied to his maple tree, but also from two of the neighbors' dogs, which raced and tumbled along behind the bicycle Wayland was riding. He spun pell-mell past the front gate and narrowly missed tipping over as he took the turn at the driveway. There was no sign of the cap he usually wore, and his first gesture upon dismounting was to flatten his curly auburn mane.

His second was to lean the cycle against the hitching post, and his third, to draw a paper bag out of his jacket pocket as he advanced cheerfully toward Aurelia and Union.

"Caramel?" he offered as he sat down between them.

"Is it yours?" Union demanded, pointing to the bicycle.

"Frank Knight at the blacksmith's let me borrow it. Belongs to his wife. When we've made some progress here, we'll knock off for a bit, and I'll show you how to get the hang of it. You will fall a few times, count on that."

The look on Union's face was such a droll mixture of bliss, eagerness, and determination, Aurelia feared he would want to "knock off" immediately, but he set to work with such goodwill, her own hands had to fly to keep up with him. Wayland pitched in, and soon the three coils of laurel garland began to resemble jungle vines.

They chatted at first, about bicycles, about caramels, fudge, and spearmint gumdrops. After a bit, as they became aware of how slowly the pile of laurel was dwindling, they concentrated more on the work, and the remarks subsided into companionable silence. By and by, they heard footsteps on the porch out toward the front of the house, and Mr. Charles's voice.

"Well, did you get him to tell you? It's that redheaded Irish one, isn't it? The schoolmarm? What is it this time? Does she still want him to become a postman?"

"She's gotten married!" Mrs. Mattie's voice shook with indignation. "To a shipping owner. A line that goes down to Cuba."

"Tarnation! Married! Just like that? With no warning?"

"Oh, who knows how long he saw it coming? If he didn't see it, he should have. He was content to paint the schoolchildren until he could afford an establishment, and they could marry and have their own. I told him she wouldn't wait forever!"

"Six years *is* forever to a pretty woman that age," Mr. Charles said. Aurelia caught a whiff of his pipe smoke. Mrs. Mattie didn't permit smoke in the house.

"But *he* paid for her teachers' college. She was hardly ahead of her students before he started helping her! It is so unfair! Poor Win!"

"Don't let him hear you say that."

"The dear fellow is half distracted by unhappiness," Mrs. Mattie almost wailed. "I knew this was coming! When I saw the picture of her peeling that lemon, I said to myself, *O-ho, that looks like a squall of Irish temperament. . . .*"

Their voices receded, and there were more footsteps — the light tap of Mrs. Mattie's neat bronze-colored leather boots going back inside, and the heavier tread of Mr. Charles going down the front steps. A moment later, they saw him strolling across the lawn to the clubhouse out by the stable to spare his wife's draperies from his tobacco fumes.

The redheaded Irish one. A squall of Irish temperament.

Aurelia stole a glance at Wayland's face.

He grinned at her.

"You know how those temperamental Irish love their lemonade," he said.

It was only a few moments later when they heard footsteps again, and the porch floorboards creaking as someone walked over to one of the rocking chairs and, presumably, sat. There were a few plunking notes, and then the banjo began to unfurl an intricate but unemphatic rendition of a minstrel tune. When the chorus came around, Mr. Winslow began to hum, then murmur the melody in a pleasant tenor.

> *"Jimmy crack corn, and I don't care,*
> *Jimmy crack corn, and I don't care. . . ."*

Heavier steps announced that the other rocker was being occupied.

"My boy, you are too down in the mouth!" pronounced a rich, rolling voice.

The banjo gently, painstakingly plunked on, the singer only raising his voice a little: "*. . . and I DON'T CARE . . . Hm, hmm, hm . . . GO A-WAY!*"

Aurelia saw that Union was so amused by this interchange, she was afraid he might laugh aloud and betray their eavesdropping. She held a finger to her lips to warn him. Probably, she realized guiltily, they ought to let on they were so nearby, hidden from the porch only by the foundation shrubbery. But it was evident that Mr. Winslow was talking to his and Mr. Charles's father. Aurelia was always interested to hear family members talking to one another. She had noticed that it was much easier to predict how parents and children in books would regard each other than in real life. This was one of the fascinating things about West Townsend: She saw more people with their families than she used to in the Sinclairs' household.

The Old Man evidently thought his son was merely singing the song's real lyrics — and that he would just as soon engage in conversation as in singing.

"Grand weather like this stimulates the metabolism, eh? Clears away the cobwebs! Time to seize the day! The season beckons!"

"*. . . and brush away the blue-tail fly.*"

"I wooed your mother in springtime, you know. We would go to the gardens, and she would paint the flowers. That's your problem, Win — you've cooped yourself up painting. You need to get out, meet stimulating company!"

"Went fly casting this very morning. Met three silver perch and a largemouth," Mr. Winslow told him, flicking his way through chord changes but giving up on singing.

"You know your sire is not one to beat around the bush. I know just the remedy you need. Been using it myself, and you see, to what good effect. What you want is Mrs. Allen's World's Hair Restorer and Zylobalsamum. 'For the old and young, for the bald and the gray' is their claim — an excellent invention. In its own way, as excellent as Charlie's varnish."

That stopped the banjo in mid-plunk.

"Mattie," Mr. Winslow yelled, "come save me from this insane old gentleman!"

Mrs. Mattie must have been just inside the door; she came outside immediately.

"I only stated the obvious," the senior Mr. Homer complained self-righteously. "You *should* seek a companion, tie the knot, and beget heirs unto the tree of thy fathers." The only time Aurelia had heard anyone speak so bluntly about marriage and begetting was when Mrs. Prentice's daughter had her baby. It had seemed fascinating and rather blessed then. But now, overheard, and with the boys sitting on either side of her, she knew she must be blushing.

"Oh, Father Homer," Mrs. Mattie said, exasperated, "he can meet as many ladies as he'd like at the party this weekend. But really, he just needs to get to his summer's painting. Don't you, Win?" she asked anxiously.

"Already started planning that," he replied. "All I have to do is hire a model, and I know who I'd like for it."

"Not the same one you painted reading the new novel?" the Old Man demanded. "I was under the impression she scuttled you."

Aurelia gasped. Oh, poor Mr. Winslow! She realized she was suddenly holding her breath, lest he say something painful.

Mr. Winslow answered in a perfectly normal voice.

"Not the same. The little girl across the street. Think you can arrange it, Mattie?"

They made one hundred feet of garlands. Mrs. Mattie paid them each seven dollars. Union fell off Wayland's bicycle nine times. He did not stay on for $47\frac{3}{4}$ seconds until after the sixth time he toppled over. After the ninth, the knees of his trousers were gone forever, as was a trifle of his own skin. He didn't mind.

Chapter 8

By the time Aurelia had hung up her bonnet, she realized gripping and twining the garlands had overworked her hands, for they ached sadly. She had planned on asking Mrs. Ellicott to show her how to repair the laundry basket; later, she expected to work on her new dress. Now, though, she felt as if a carryall had driven over her fingers.

Mrs. Ellicott had heard about the laurel labors, and was surprised and pleased at Union's dedication to the task. Looking at Aurelia's poor, swollen hands, she kindly ordered her just to sit and watch how to prepare the willow for weaving. The withes had been soaking in the rain barrel overnight. When she had peeled the bark off the wands, she made a hot tea from the shreds of it, for Aurelia to dip flannel into, to wrap her hands.

"Miss Calantha taught me that the first time I tried basketry," Mrs. Ellicott remarked, settling into a comfortable, companionable manner. "She has always been so clever at everything. Some might think," she went on, glancing over her spectacles at Aurelia, then back at the white withe she was trimming, "a woman with so much book learning might not be interested in the domestic virtues. But Miss Calantha has real talent in useful handicrafts, besides being conversant in foreign languages and literature."

"When she recommends a book," Aurelia acknowledged, "it is always the sort I like. What languages does she know? Can she read Latin? I might like to learn."

Mrs. Ellicott nodded emphatically as she cut away the bitten-off handle.

"Oh, yes — Latin, Italian, Portuguese, German, French. She even knows some Mandarin, because Captain Crofoot, her father, was a clipper captain. They had the most beautiful shelves full of blue-and-white porcelain! When I was a little older than you, they helped get me enrolled in the Female Seminary. I could speak English, but I could write only French. Miss Calantha was so patient with me, finally I passed the examination."

The flannel had cooled, so Aurelia dipped her hands again into the basin.

"Has she lived in that same sixteen-sided house all her life?" she asked. Such solidity was a novel thought to Aurelia. She watched as Mrs. Ellicott began to weave the first new course of willow along the raw, damaged edge.

"She went away for a while after her good mother passed on and her father retired. She did not get on well with him.

That is why we have Cicero, I think." Mrs. Ellicott laughed. "She said it was because of the time he ate the covers off all the books in the parlor. But she could have kept him in a cage, as we do. No, I am quite sure it was really because the old blue thing sounds just like Captain Crofoot."

Aurelia was somewhat shocked to hear Mrs. Ellicott speak so of the dead. In the Egyptian novel she had begun reading, Aurelia had learned that the ancient people believed the shades of the dead went to live in the western desert. She wondered if they supposed dead sea captains went there, too, and people who died in shipwrecks. She wondered, how far west could a spirit go?

After school on Friday, Aurelia was tending to Uncle Adams, unsnarling his rope where he had tangled himself in the viburnaum bushes on the shady side of the house, when Elima and Livia descended upon Amity for their usual tea and gossip. Through the open parlor window, she heard Elima making what Aurelia thought an overly dramatic announcement. (That was another thing Aurelia found trying about Elima: She gushed.)

"You will never guess the delicious news I just heard from Mother! Mittie, you sly thing, you should have told us!"

"I am sure I don't know what you have heard," Amity answered eagerly.

"That your good looks have caught an artist's eye! Mother

ran into Mrs. Homer today and learned that Mr. Homer's brother wishes to paint your portrait!"

Aurelia felt miffed. It wasn't surprising, though, that a painter would be looking for rich girls whose parents could afford to pay for their daughters' loveliness to be immortalized in oils. Miss Amity had golden brown hair, and eyes big and dark as a fawn's. Aurelia supposed a gilt-framed portrait of her would eventually hang in the parlor.

"Why, he is becoming rather a prominent painter," Livia approved. "Sitting for him might be quite the thing. If he does well enough on the picture of you, perhaps Papa will decide to hire him to paint *me*."

"Well, I have heard nothing of this," Amity declared, "but perhaps he saw me when Mother and I went calling on Mrs. Mattie. I was wearing my new bonnet with the pale blue veil and black egret tips. It is rather eye-catching."

Especially those egret tips, Aurelia thought. Once she had stood near enough that a toss of Amity's head had indeed caught her in the eye with the stylish plumage.

"I hope you realize Mr. Frederic W. might be jealous," Elima pointed out with evident relish. "Of the whole gallery admiring you, when you are all the rage in Boston."

"Nonsense," Livia said. "It takes a good deal of time, but posing for a portrait is a noble endeavor. I always applaud fine art. It is a sign of good breeding to appreciate it."

Aurelia was of the opinion (instilled perhaps by Mrs.

Prentice) that it was a sign of good breeding when one's horse won a race; and, decidedly, a sign of good manners not to brag about one's own good breeding as if one's parents had four feet apiece.

When Mrs. Mattie and Mr. Winslow came to call on Mrs. Ellicott twenty minutes later, however, it became clear that Amity was not the "Ellicott girl" he had meant.

"Beg pardon. Misunderstanding," he said gruffly. "The one I want has dark hair."

"Oh, for goodness' sake, Winslow," Mrs. Mattie said, sensitive to the disappointment on Amity's face. "You didn't say that before."

"HAUL IN THE STUNS'LS!" Cicero suddenly squawked. Everybody jumped.

"I regret the error," Mr. Winslow said patiently. "But the model I need must have dark hair. She was out in Ash Swamp, picking flowers with her brothers?"

"Aurelia," Amity realized, horror-struck. "With *my* brother. And that Irish boy!"

"Winslow, honestly," Mrs. Mattie said gently, "you see everything and you still manage not to see anything. Albertine, is Aurelia here? Winslow, Aurelia is Mrs. Ellicott's . . . staff. She's hired help." To Mrs. Ellicott, she added, "Winslow pays his models for their time, of course."

✼   ✼   ✼

"Yes. That one," Mr. Winslow Homer said. Aurelia felt herself blush. She had been upstairs, using Mrs. Ellicott's sewing machine to join the bodice and skirt of her new dress. Mr. Winslow caught her eye, but she couldn't tell whether or not he was smiling. "Where's your pickerel retriever today?" he demanded.

"He's tied up at the moment, sir," Aurelia answered politely.

"He's not *her* dog, he's *our* dog," Amity protested. Mrs. Ellicott touched her arm.

"REEF THE TOPGALLANTS!" Cicero screeched.

"When I saw you in Ash Swamp," Mr. Winslow was saying directly to Aurelia, "I was reminded of a bit of work I started as a watercolor last summer and would like to work up as an oil. If you will permit me . . ." He looked inquiringly at Mrs. Ellicott, then laid a black leatherboard portfolio across his knees, opened it, and withdrew a painting of a shepherd girl leaning wearily against a massive tree. She was wearing a broad curtain bonnet that billowed like a spinnaker, catching all the sunshine at her back, so her face and the whole front of her figure were in shadow.

"Who is that girl?" she asked. Aurelia wondered if it was the sweetheart who scuttled him.

"Oh, the model — a schoolgirl. Did that sketch up in Ulster County . . ." he murmured aside to Mrs. Mattie. "Used to do studies of the schoolchildren at recess."

"And I'd be standing like that, leaning on a tree?"

"No. I'll change that. Your posture is better than that girl's was."

"You mean, I'll have to stand still for — how long?"

"An hour at a time. With three breaks. One hour a day in the right weather."

"Without anything to lean on?" Aurelia still thought it didn't sound comfortable.

"No, we'll do something about that."

Something Elima had said was nagging at Aurelia. What had she said? *"Of the whole gallery . . . when you are all the rage in Boston . . ."* What if Mr. E. Hancock went to a gallery? Would he recognize her? Would he know the painting had been made in West Townsend and come after her?

Aurelia studied the watercolor. She did not think she could have recognized that schoolgirl if she met her on the street.

"I don't have that kind of slat-curtain bonnet," she said cautiously.

"I have the hat and apron. A costume, really — the Old World shepherdess, Mary and her little lamb. Some critics don't favor . . . er . . . purity . . . when it's in straw hats and boots and freckled, straight-haired Yankee urchins. I don't give two pins for the critics, but I want folks to like my paintings: I have to sell them."

✻   ✻   ✻

Mr. Winslow was sitting in the oval-backed armchair. He was tipping his head ever so slightly, looking at Aurelia as if he were consulting the window light. Aurelia realized the raw-edged right sleeve of her new dress was in her pocket, along with her pincushion and thimble. She also realized she had pushed her hair back out of her eyes when Mrs. Ellicott rang the bell for her, but she had not combed it before running downstairs. She thought she must look awfully flyaway. Flyaway and lumpy, in her spotty blue-and-yellow everyday calico whose colors had run like a naughty child the first time she washed it and every time since.

Wayland also sometimes looked at her intently like this, but when Wayland looked directly at her, into her eyes, she felt he was fond of her, and she saw he thought her pretty. (Sometimes, though, he looked past her, and she thought *perhaps* he was thinking of things she reminded him of — things he wanted to tell her about. Words of poems, maybe.)

When Mr. Winslow Homer looked, he looked her in the eye, but not for long. He was a proper gentleman — perhaps shy, she thought. She had the impression she might have been Niagara Falls or a picturesque lighthouse. His expression was not tender, it was rather abstract.

Mr. Ellicott scarcely ever looked at her at all. The fewer the people in the house and the quieter, the better he liked an evening. He preferred not to mix with employees.

When Union looked at her, it was as if she could hear

him thinking the next page of his own inner story: *He will be there in 382 seconds! By Jove, we are saved then!*

"Excuse me — is this a scarf or . . . ? May I take a look at that color?" Mr. Winslow asked.

Embarrassed, Aurelia handed over her scrap of sewing. She had buttoned on the yellow cuff to help adjust the lining and the lace oversleeve so they wouldn't bunch up.

"Is that your sewing, Aurelia?" Mrs. Mattie asked kindly. "How nicely you do it."

"The housekeeper where I was before taught me," Aurelia told her. "It's my dress for Decoration Day. I am afraid it won't be done until the last minute, so I should not —"

"We don't need to start until June — I must go to Fitchburg for some of the paint I need. Wear that frock for the sittings, if you would be so kind," Mr. Winslow said as he put away the watercolor sketch. "Without cuffs. They're the same color as that basket you were carrying — I prefer you leave them off. But I would like you to bring that same basket with you, as well, when you pose. And we shall need someone to hold the brushes — you may invite whomever seems right for the post, and I shall see how that works."

Having said all this, he stood up briskly and began shaking hands so Mrs. Mattie had no choice but to follow suit, fluttering off into little hand pats and "My dears" for all.

"ALTER COURSE," Cicero commanded, "FOUR POINTS TO STARBOARD!"

Union was sitting on the front steps, drawing with a stub of pencil in an old copybook. The drawing was an elaborate one, spread across two pages, and involving velocipedes and hot-air balloons, as well as a Bayliss-Thomas only slightly shorter than the Baptist Church steeple past which it was streaking.

Mr. Winslow paused as he went down the steps and peered at Union's panorama.

"Good perspective," he remarked. "But, look, you moved your focal point when you did this side. The horse is jolly good — is that Grant, there?"

"I reckon," Union managed, unspeakably embarrassed at the attention.

"Looks just like him. Tipsy."

"Oh, for goodness' sake, Winslow," Mrs. Mattie scolded.

Mrs. Ellicott sent Aurelia to Howe's to buy gelatin, for she had decided at the last minute to make an orange charlotte for dessert. It was Amity's favorite.

At Howe's, Livia was studying the array of scissors and shears Fred Wagner had displayed on the counter. Livia was trying them on scraps of newspaper and worsted.

". . . poor dear," she was saying when Aurelia walked in. "She is convinced it is her complexion or her tallness that doesn't suit. And what could I tell her? Of course, he could paint over her blemishes easily; but she *would* carry on. And after all, artists are such odd sorts, you know, there's no accounting for *their* taste."

"Miss Amity?" Aurelia ventured, looking into Miss Ellicott's room later. She had thought of bringing her the mixing bowl and spoon to lick when the charlotte had gone into the ice chest to chill, but at the last moment decided it might seem disrespectful.

"What do you want?" was the ungracious response. Miss Amity was sitting next to her Hadley chest, going through the linens she had laid by for that happy day in the future when she would, herself, set up housekeeping.

"I know why he can't bear to paint you."

The look of hatred and resentment Amity shot at Aurelia almost blew her down.

"Can't *bear* to!"

"His sweetheart had lighter hair than mine. Like yours is lighter. Hers was red, though. But she jilted him."

"Oh, you spy on other people's secrets do you?" Amity said coldly.

"I wasn't spying. But don't you see? He doesn't want to paint a sweetheart. He just wants to paint a . . . just a plain girl. A girl who has to work. A shadowy girl."

"Go wash Uncle Adams," Amity told her. "He rolled in something while you were talking to your artist friend."

Aurelia gave the spoon and bowl to Union.

Chapter 9

When Aurelia told Miss Calantha about the painting, the librarian knew just where to find the journals in which Mr. Winslow's paintings had been reviewed. Others in town, she hinted, had wanted to keep up with the art world.

"The remark about Yankee urchins was made by Mr. Henry James, the stuck-up thing." Miss Calantha laughed a dry, indignant little laugh Aurelia found irresistible. "The *Evening Post* didn't like him to paint an Irish model."

"This is not the Paris Salon," Aurelia remarked, feeling very sophisticated after skimming over the magazine articles. "I should think he can paint what he likes, in America," Aurelia said. Wayland was not in the library this Saturday morning, so she went on. "Why, I know girls," she said quietly, though there was no one there in the library room except the two of them, "who cannot be respectful toward their own neighbors and classmates from the north end of town."

Miss Calantha was putting Aurelia's returned books back on the sorting table.

"Now, that's too bad," she said with a sigh. "You would think the worst of the old ways would be the first to go, as the world progresses." She paused, one book clasped momentarily to her heart as if it held some cherished tale. "To have an Irish beau can be a moment of . . . poetry . . . in one's life, Miss Sandborn. I assure you, base prejudice leads only to . . . loss. Tragic loss. That the opinions of others should curtail one's most inspired endeavors . . . it should be unthinkable!"

She looked down at the book she was clutching so fervently, and discovered the issue of *St. Nicholas* with *The Peterkin Papers* excerpts in it. She laughed her dry little laugh again.

"They are only opinions," Aurelia said with a shrug. "Anyway, I quite like the painting Mr. Winslow Homer showed me. But Miss Amity is vexed with me, and I am not sure about Mrs. Ellicott."

"There are reasons parents are indulgent . . . or not," Miss Calantha reflected. "What would Agamemnon and Solomon John do?" Miss Calantha asked, referring to characters in *The Peterkin Papers*.

"Well, they'd probably cut the hole in the ceiling first, and *then* ask advice of the lady from Philadelphia," Aurelia said, thinking, *I used to ask Mrs. Prentice.* "But who do I know who's from Philadelphia?" As she said the words, she wondered if, in fact, she were from Philadelphia, herself. The *Aspiration* had sailed from there.

"You'll just have to be your own lady from Philadelphia,"

Miss Calantha said. "You will have to not forget your own common sense."

Saturday evening, the broad, elm-shaded avenue that was Main Street exchanged its usual log wagons for stylish carriages, gentlemen in tall silk hats, and ladies in elaborate silk gowns. Meanwhile, the Ellicotts' house was overrun with Amity's classmates. Besides Livia and Elima, a dozen other girls gossiped in the parlor and giggled in the passageway, shrieked on the stairs, pouted in the vestibule, and nibbled at the buffet. Aurelia flitted hither and yon with sandwiches, ices, and mint tea.

Elima's dramatic announcement on this occasion concerned a telegram Laurence Boutelle had delivered to her mother.

"I shall not say what was in it, only that it is something most fortunate going to happen to someone we know. And not who you'd expect. But I wish Ma wouldn't go by Beulah. I was perfectly mortified to hear Laurence saying 'Mrs. Beulah Worthy.' Her real name is Bonny. I think it's twice as nice, but Ma doesn't think it's elegant enough."

A girl named Sarah Meadows patted Elima on the shoulder.

"But your name is so much more unusual," she consoled her.

"You don't know how lucky you are, to have a unique

old family name instead of a common one," Mary Taylor told her.

So went the girlish chatter. Aurelia carried in cheese straws and macaroons. The twilight had gone sapphire and the evening star was lit; the gaslights, likewise, starred the lilac-scented world. Aurelia had just brought in plates of strawberry shortcake when the girls heard a sweet melody arising from handsome voices under the window. Some of the lads had been plotting a May concert for the ladies, and now their impromptu glee club delivered a spirited selection.

Starting with the sweetest *a cappella* "In the Sweet By and By," they soon roused everyone's feelings with "Wake Nicodemus." Then the real fun began, for the fellows pushed one of their number forward to sing solo in front of their softly murmured harmony of wordless chords, and when he sang "Afton Water," the girls giggled behind the draperies, for his tribute to "my Mary" was understood to mean Mary Taylor. Likewise, "Annie Laurie" by another swain was awarded to Annabelle Eno, and Sarah Meadows was much teased when the crooners rendered "Sally in Our Alley."

"You see," Elima said in resignation, "there are no songs about Elima or Livia or Amity, so no one has anything to say to us."

In fact, the fellows seemed to be finishing with "The Sword of Bunker Hill," knowing that any neighbors they had distressed with their nocturnal warblings would be assuaged by the sound of that moving old anthem.

"Oh, but, listen," Elima said, as the wandering minstrels retreated, still singing. "'The Sands o' Dee' — how clever!"

"What do you mean?" Sally demanded.

"It's another one about Mary," Aurelia said under her breath, catching the words, but alarmed nonetheless. She had heard the sad, old song before, and knew what came next:

> *The western wind was wild and dank with foam . . .*
> *Oh, is it weed, or fish, or floating hair,*
> *A tress of golden hair,*
> *A drowned maiden's hair*
> *Above the nets at sea?*

She used to hate it when Mr. E. Hancock would sit pounding out the melody on the quaking old spinet in the drawing room, and singing in what he said was a Scottish accent.

Another verse arose in Aurelia's memory, rose like a tall wave.

> *The abyss enveloped me; seaweed clung about my head. . . .*

"A tribute to Miss *Sand*born?" Elima purred. "Wonder whose idea that was."

"It isn't about me," Aurelia said faintly. "It's for Mary."

Could anybody possibly know she was a castaway?

At the library, Aurelia returned Edward Lear and the *Peterkins*. She had checked out *Life on the Mississippi* and *The Odyssey*. She was still reading *Uarda*.

"Those ancient Egyptians had such complicated ideas about heaven," she had remarked to Miss Calantha.

"If only the spirits departed *would* walk into the room and eat the dinner we'd cook for them — if only we could! — and tell us where they wander among the Elysian fields!" Miss Calantha had mused — rather sadly, Aurelia had thought.

But then the librarian's wistful face had brightened.

"I have been reading a most fascinating book," Miss Calantha confided, "issued by the Guides of the Inner Light Society. It is a comfort and an inspiration, and Madame Czemunie, who wrote it, claims to be regularly in contact with the liberated — that means 'enlightened' — spirits and guides. She recommends a method."

"What do you mean, 'a method'?" Aurelia asked. On the whole, she thought she preferred Egyptologists to ghosts.

"She is very modern. I think it has something to do with magnetism and electrical currents. She has conducted such experiments before."

Mrs. Prentice had thought well of spiritism, automatic writing, magnetic channels in the ether and what all. Aurelia was not sure whether she herself thought ghosts were scientific, or just fairy stories. Both ghosts and angels were in the Scriptures. She felt her own mama was more like an angel than a ghost. Did angels come to séances?

"Experiments?" Aurelia asked dubiously. "Pulling departed spirits out of heaven the way a magnet finds nails spilled in the sawdust?"

Miss Calantha laughed. "To hear her tell it, it is just as natural."

Aurelia wondered what it would be like if it weren't her mama who came. What if it were the man in her locket? Or what if it were President Lincoln?

"Do you send for a particular spirit?" she asked. "Or just see who calls on you?"

"Well, now, I am not sure. Both, I expect."

Decoration Day was humid and hot already by ten o'clock in the morning. Aurelia's new dress was finished. She knew all the words of "The Blue and the Gray," and all week, she had practiced how to say the lines. The stanzas were so repetitive, she tended to lose her place. But she had at least, finally, overcome the temptation to singsong to herself, "*By the fwoe of the inwand wiver. . . .*"

There was to be a parade, with the town band playing. The veterans of the Grand Army of the Republic would march in uniform, and wagons and carriages decorated with flags, bunting, and flowers would carry the town leaders up to Hillside Cemetery to lay wreaths on the graves of Townsend's beloved heroes. Aurelia was to ride on a white-draped wagon for the ones speaking during the memorial service. Wayland's place was on the senior-class wagon, on a bench under a rickety pergola made to look like marble swagged with ivy: Wayland, Laurence, and Cornelius, the three top scholars, rode in the place of honor, surrounded by classmates displaying large scrolls bearing the words *Knowledge, Science, Philosophy, Wisdom, Liberty,* and *Progress.*

"They're not all up there in the cemetery," Wayland said to Aurelia as they stood with the rest of the milling crowd, waiting for the signal to take their places in line and strike up the band. "We reckon my uncle Julian is buried somewhere in Tennessee."

"Is Mrs. Farwell's husband up there?" Aurelia asked.

"He is, but his head's not," Union told her with an air of casual disinterest. "Mithradates Gleason says his father's helper said it wasn't in the coffin the train brought back."

In the library, Miss Calantha had shown Aurelia Mr. Winslow's pictures in *Harper's Weekly.* Season after season through the years of the war, he had tramped through mud and destruction with the boys in blue, sharing their campfire coffee and hardtack, watching them clean their muskets and darn their socks and bring cups of water to the wounded. He had watched them fire those same muskets and slash out with their elegant sabers, seen them blasted backward off their stumbling horses and trampled by human beings mad with blood. He had drawn them in plain, black ink, and then he had begun to paint them in their true, smoky colors.

Mrs. Fussburton, Mrs. Adams, and Mrs. Twitchell bustled around, distributing bouquets of lilac and dogwood to the high school girls, and bunches of violets and Johnny-jump-ups to the little ones. As a speaker, Aurelia received a wreath of daphne and lily of the valley to wear on her hair. She had to ask Miss Calantha to hold her bonnet for her through the festivities. She had no hairpins, though, and the wreath kept slipping. Mrs. Worthy noticed her discomfort and dug two pins into her scalp to hold the wreath in place. Aurelia accepted the gesture with mingled gratitude and pain.

The fifes, drums, and bugles thrilled them all; even the horses pulling the celebrants pranced in the air of noble valor that hovered over the old Massachusetts Common.

The mayor spoke. Congressman Adams spoke. Mrs. Adams and Mrs. Fussburton spoke. Mr. Fussburton spoke, and his son, Captain Fussburton of the 33rd Massachusetts Volunteers spoke, recalling the local men lost at Fredericksburg, at Chancellorsville, at Gettysburg and Lookout Mountain, at Laurel Mountain and Missionary Ridge, and at Cedar Creek and Resaca. Sergeant Shaw of the 19th Army Corps spoke of his own men, and of his cousin Colonel Robert Shaw's 54th, the tragic and glorious regiment of free black soldiers who laid their lives on the altar of abolition, where President Lincoln himself ultimately laid his own.

When it was time, Aurelia's poem went by smoothly and was over soon, though Aurelia did not speak too fast.

> *These in the robings of glory,*
> *Those in the gloom of defeat,*
> *All, with the battle-blood gory,*
> *In the dusk of eternity meet:*
> *Under the sod and the dew,*
> *Waiting the judgment-day;*
> *Under the laurel, the Blue,*
> *Under the willow, the Gray.*

Mr. Winslow was there, sitting with Mrs. Mattie, Mr. Charles, and Mr. Charles Senior. Their heads were bowed, but Mr. Winslow was looking around, a thoughtful, somber expression on his face, even as he discreetly fanned himself with his boater.

> *So, when the summer calleth*
> *On forest and field of grain. . . .*

Aurelia saw where Mrs. Farwell was standing, a pillar in black, by a simple slate stone draped on this day with the red, white, and blue. There was a tiny limestone marker set in the moss beside it. The air was hot and still, full of the odor of the glum cedars and weeping beeches.

> *Love and tears for the Blue,*
> *Tears and love for the Gray.*

When she finished her piece, Aurelia walked away from the speakers' platform feeling a little light-headed, and placed her wreath of white blossom on Private Farwell's grave. Then she went back and stood with the rest of the students. The sun was exceedingly hot on her uncovered hair. She wondered if what she'd done was all right.

Mr. Ithamar Sawtelle, the town historian, spoke. Mr. Miletus Gleason stepped up onto the podium and took great pains with his elocution, introducing himself nervously and slowly. He recited a poem by Walt Whitman. Aurelia could tell he'd been working on his enunciation.

> *O Captain! my Captain! our fearful trip is done . . .*

The poem was about President Lincoln, but Aurelia was having a hard time listening. She was so warm, too warm . . . and standing was so . . . tedious . . . so heavy. . . .

Here Captain! dear father! . . .
It is some dream that on the deck,
You've fallen cold and dead. . . .

The wave of darkness swallowed her.

Darkness and red weighed heavy on her eyelids. She was on the ground. They were all around her. She should open her eyes. Would, in a moment. She was rocking in the boat. She was lying in the graveyard and many were around her. Did that mean? . . .

A strong arm came round her shoulders, lifted her head off the dirt.

"She needs air! Let her breathe!" Wayland said. He was beside her, helping her to sit up. She opened her eyes and saw his face above her, full of tender concern.

Mrs. Ellicott was there, too, and Miss Calantha, and Mrs. Worthy.

"Did you eat any breakfast this morning?" Mrs. Ellicott was asking. Suddenly, Aurelia's nose was full of ammonia fumes as a bottle of smelling salts was wielded.

"A little," Aurelia managed, pushing away the salts. "Milk. I was hemming . . ." Her skirt was twisted under her — there. She found Mrs. Worthy's two hairpins and held them out to her. "Thank you . . ." She closed her eyes, and they thought she had blacked out again. She had not.

She had heard Amity's voice somewhere nearby. Too loud. "Just hungry for attention . . ."

And Livia: "Well, now she has that pushy Irish boy making himself familiar, what more can she ask?"

Later, back in her little sleeping-porch room with the oilcloth shades pulled down, with a cold compress on her forehead and a glass of iced tea at hand, it occurred to Aurelia. Since Mrs. Prentice went away — more than a year ago, now — Wayland was the first human being who had put a kind arm around her.

Chapter 10

"Do you possess a pair of white stockings?" Then, hearing what he'd said, Mr. Winslow amended, "I beg your pardon. It seems a personal question, but it is merely artistic. Dark stockings make too big a blot in the lower portion of the work."

"I have my Sunday pair. I could wear them," Aurelia said.

"No, don't turn your head," he reminded her. "Put it back where it was. Slide your nosetip about a half an inch back. Good. Stick your chin out just a . . . good! Stop!"

He was sitting on a camp stool, a block of sketching paper on his knees, and he was scribbling deftly with charcoal. Every so often, he glanced at the watercolor of the weary shepherdess, and then at Aurelia.

"You're not fatigued, are you?" he asked vaguely, smudging some line or other with his little finger, then absentmindedly rubbing the residue off on his trouser leg.

"After this little while posing? Not a bit," Aurelia assured him.

"But, let us just try this: Lean back a little against the wall. Just for a trifle of support. If you were tired, would that help? Some days, you will be tired, you know. We will always be working with afternoon light."

"I'm leaning. Does it look as if I'm leaning?"

"Not much. That's good, if you need respite."

"I'm not going to faint again, sir," Aurelia said, slightly nettled. "That was only because I had no sunbonnet. Or parasol. And I certainly do, now."

"Nonetheless. Don't want the hens after me for picking on you."

The "hens" were Mrs. Mattie and Mrs. Ellicott, who were sitting across the yard on the porch, enjoying cool tumblers of lemonade, which Aurelia envied.

She and Mr. Winslow were by the little bridge where the Squannicook passed under the road and a canal nipped around the back of the Homers' property. Mr. Winslow liked to paint in the open air. He had found a place where the laurel leaned over the weathered gate and foamed up behind the unmortared stones of the old farm wall. He had taken Aurelia's arm as if he were escorting her into a ballroom and walked her over to the exact place where he wanted her to pose, then gently twirled her around to stand —

"Just . . . like . . . that. Yes."

She had hoped he'd say something about her dress, and he had, but not anything like what she'd expected.

"Nice eye for color, miss. Now, you'll see, it's just the color we'll get — here, put this thing on" — the "thing" being a fancy pinafore with eyelet-point lace trim — "yes! Just the color of the shadows on the white. Perfect."

He fussed over the bonnet endlessly, tying, loosening, folding back the brim, puffing it out, tweaking it here and there. The primping was not exactly womanish — he was like a draper arranging new window hangings. She found herself gazing up at his face, while he bent his attention everywhere else but into her gaze. He had a nice, strong chin, she decided. And he looked as though he had recently evened out his mustache, for it was as neat as any of the new paintbrushes purchased in Fitchburg. The little squint lines around his eyes made him look older up close than he did from what Aurelia thought of as a normal distance.

He smelled of pipe tobacco rather more than of tobacco smoke, and of . . . coffee . . . applesauce or maple sugar, she couldn't decide which; and there was something else more sharply exotic, balmy. . . .

She thought it must be Mrs. Allen's Zylobalsamum.

After a quarter of an hour, Mr. Winslow told Aurelia to "let up for a few moments" to refresh herself. Mrs. Mattie strolled over with the yearned-for lemonade pitcher. Father Homer had meanwhile appeared and took the opportunity to join his son. As soon as Mrs. Mattie went back to Mrs. Ellicott, he began complaining about his daughter-in-law's hard-heartedness.

"She entirely overlooked my requirement of pure shaving water, and let that little fellow with the French name tip over the rain barrel into the asparagus bed!"

"Father, it was breeding skeeters. It's going to rain again tomorrow, anyway. Your whiskers can last that long."

"And that lemonade has no heft to it at all. Must've been made from one meager lemon, and we can afford to be less frugal than *that*, I think!"

Mr. Winslow sipped from his glass. "Plenty of heft, Father. Just no Holland gin."

"Winslow, my boy, I shall always regret that New York has made a cynic of you. You know I wear the White Ribbon — I have taken my temperance vow ne'er to indulge in spiritous beverages. Mattie says I ought to go home to Mother."

"You should. Mother must be feeling quite dull without you. And we need the bedroom space here. I have a guest due in for a couple of days." Mr. Winslow had polished off his lemonade. Aurelia looked inquiringly at him. A guest?

"Who? One of the crowned heads of Europe?" Father Homer asked.

Mr. Winslow began poking around in his workbox, picking out pieces of charcoal the size he liked.

"Army pal I ran into in Fitchburg. Says he's going up to

Maine when he's done here, so I told him to come by, catch up on things — perhaps later in the season, we'll go up to the Willows and do some fishing together."

"Another angler, eh?" Father Homer said, without a trace of his usual enthusiasm. "The sparkle of your dear mother's conversation does indeed begin to assert its old siren-sweet inducement."

"Good," Mr. Winslow said, taking up his sketch pad again. "Aurelia?"

Aurelia gazed along the ferny line of the wall. She could not turn her head, or look very far up or down. She couldn't check on the already drooping cluster of blossoms hanging over the edge of her basket, lest the shade cast by her bonnet should move. If she forgot herself and did look down, or slouch, or shift her feet, Mr. Winslow made a quiet, disappointed little sound and murmured, "Shadow, miss."

At first, she found herself worrying about how big or small various parts of her would appear to Mr. Winslow. If she blushed, wouldn't he see it immediately? Thinking of it, she *did* blush; Mr. Winslow just kept drawing, without any comment. After half an hour of posing, she began to feel that he was not really looking at her at all — he was looking at the shadows and light. She was not what he was drawing — she was more like the paper on which he was drawing; what the sun and shadow were drawing on her, he was copying. By that time, her self-consciousness came and went — but was, in any event, no longer painful.

The wall was an old one. These stones had been in place a hundred, perhaps two hundred years. They were rough, rounded, keg-sized stones, most of them granite, a few with streaks of marble showing, or a glint of mica where the moss had gotten scraped away. Flotsam of ancient glaciers, they were patchy with bluish lichens, and here or there a bush or sapling had grown right up through the middle of the wall where a bird or a red squirrel had dropped a seed or an acorn in a crevice, and it had never been disturbed.

"What will you do when the flowers are gone?" Aurelia asked Mr. Winslow. Already, many blossoms had fallen — the rain, when it came, would finish them.

"I already painted a few studies. I have what I need," Mr. Winslow murmured. "I shall remember."

"Let's take a look," Mr. Winslow said at the end of an hour. He propped up his sketch, leaning it on the stone wall next to where Aurelia was holding the basket, and looked at it and her together. Because of his mustache, she could not see whether he was pleased. He set the watercolor of the weary shepherdess next to the new charcoal version.

The big tree had disappeared from the composition now, and the girl at its center, although a shorter girl, was a bigger part of the picture. The curve was gone from her posture: She was as unbowed as a mast. The laurel bushes were not so tall and dense as in the old watercolor, and they seemed to have more white patches of flowers. There were clouds in the sky above them. The smudge of shadows eclipsed most of her face. No one could look at the sketch Mr. Winslow had made, Aurelia thought, and recognize her for who she was.

"I see," she said. "It didn't need the tree trunk. And the circle of shadows makes rather a blot around her." She studied the two pictures as she untied the big bonnet (which had not been tied in the first version). "And I expect my flower basket's more fun to paint than the crook she was leaning on."

"Precisely my notion," Mr. Winslow said. His cheery voice now made it clear he was pleased. He reached into his pocket and took out a little square, folded-leather coin purse, from which he extracted a silver dollar. Half a week's pay for an hour of standing still, doing nothing! Or was it her week's pay for modeling, in advance? Either way, Aurelia thought, Mr. Winslow was an exceptionally liberal soul. "My thanks, missie," he said kindly. "Tomorrow, at the same time. Tomorrow we start in color."

"I shall wear my white stockings, sir," Aurelia promised.

But the next morning, the sky was gray and brooding. Hoping for the best, Aurelia wore her white stockings, but it did not look as if it would clear before afternoon.

And really, despite the wonderful silver spondulix in the

slide-top box, she was rather relieved not to have to pose. School was half-days because it was final examination week, and she wanted to go to the library, in case Wayland was there. Seniors had taken their last tests already — the graduation ceremony was to be held on the upcoming Sunday. She had not seen him since Decoration Day, and she had begun to worry that he had heard and been hurt by Livia's taunting remark. She had reluctantly decided, though, that she needed as much time as she could find to work on her mathematics.

Union, however, was of a mind to loiter near the screen porch where she was studying. He, too, seemed overcast and brooding. First he was outside, pacing around, whipping randomly at the mock-orange and lilac bushes with his hoop stick. Then he was inside, fidgeting with a small paper sack, opening it, rolling the top closed, opening it again with a rattle, closing it, and putting it into his pocket.

"Union, I'm studying."

"If someone gives you something you like," he began meditatively, "and you think it's . . . well, a bribe — but they don't really *say* — and you don't *promise* not to tell what they don't want you to — but you think you ought to — can you eat the gumdrops?"

Aurelia closed her mathematics book with her finger holding the place.

"Why do you reckon you ought to tell?"

"Because there's a snake in the grass. Two, in fact." Union

opened the sack of sweets and stared into it with longing. "Is Mittie home?" he asked cautiously.

"She's at the Worthys', studying with Elima."

"Well, I know where Twitch is today."

"I heard her tell Amity she was to be fitted for her cotillion gown."

Union shrugged, and shook two gumdrops into his hand. He put one in his mouth and held the other out to Aurelia. His hand was not visibly dirty, so she took it.

"Not unless Fred Wagner is her dressmaker. Not unless he had his arm around her waist to measure for her sash."

Aurelia chewed her gumdrop and swallowed.

"Laurence is the one who's sweet on Amity," she said. "He's forever telling me to give her his regards."

"Want to know!" Union said, evidently much relieved. "See if I don't turn that to some benefit."

When Amity returned from Elima's, she was surprised to find a pretty nosegay of lilac and mock-orange on the front step. The little card attached read, *A. E., with the compliments of an admirer. (Not F. W.)* She did not recognize the laboriously perfect handwriting as her brother's.

Chapter 11

It rained great guns. For the first time in weeks, it poured, and the sky was lavish with lightning. Aurelia ran outside at one point to get Uncle Adams' dish from his favorite spot under the viburnum. She carried an umbrella, but alas! — she forgot about the white stockings and the new coat of blacking she'd given her boots before going over to Mrs. Mattie's to pose. One clap of thunder was so close, the noise staggered her, and she stepped directly into a puddle so deep it went over the top of her boot. The boots were ruined, she realized to her dismay when she tried to dry them. Even though they weren't of the best quality, replacing them would cost her most of her savings. And the stockings! . . .

She wondered when, or if, Mr. Winslow would pay her again. She was not sure it was ladylike to ask.

Friday morning, Aurelia had her geography examination, her last; and the sun came out. She was relieved to be done with school for the year. When the week's wash was on the line, she went over to the Homers'.

The laurel bushes had lost the last tatters of bloom, but Mr. Winslow hummed like a contented bee as he moved about, setting up his camp chair and worktable, laying out his array of watercolors, cups, and a pitcher of water. He lined up his brushes, from an inch wide down to finicky points of only two or three fine, red sable hairs.

"Today we do the color sketch," he explained as he steered her into her place by the wall. "Watercolors are, for the most part, transparent, and they dry very quickly. So it is of utmost importance today that you hold your course steady and do not even glance away. Imagine you are a cigar store Cherokee, or a ship's figurehead. You look very charming — we shall have a top-notch painting, by and by. Yes. Absolutely." He stood back. "Thank you for remembering the stockings," he added as he settled himself and began mixing his first pale blue wash.

The rain-soaked ground steamed in the sunshine. All along the wall, the grass had suddenly frothed up drifts of blue-violet bugle and snow-white quaker-ladies, and a few yards from where Aurelia stood like a statue, a spike of pipsissewa flirted with a tiny azure butterfly. It began to get hot. By suppertime, the mosquitoes that had been vanquished by the days of downpour would be replenished; but for now, Aurelia noticed thankfully, they were lying low.

When they had taken their first break and then resumed work, Aurelia saw from the corner of her eye a bearded gentleman hesitantly approaching from the house.

"It's all right, Joe," Mr. Winslow hailed him. "You sat by me on many a harder day than this — I don't generally invite sightseers, but don't let Mattie discourage *you*."

"Well, you have a better-looking model today than in the old cavalry days," his guest said. Mr. Winslow laughed.

"And not one swinging a sword around so picturesquely, my neck's at risk! Miss Ellicott, Mr. Grunreiter. Formerly, Corporal — don't move a muscle, now, missie," he said, before Aurelia could correct his error by saying Sandborn.

"I shall sit back here, out of the way," his old army chum assured him. It sounded as though he sat on the gate, off to her left where he wouldn't distract the eye of either artist or model. Aurelia was surprised to hear a German accent to his warm, comfortable baritone. "But I want to inform you of my itinerary. I shall leave on the Pepperell train and wire you when I know when I'll be returning. I . . . have a letter to deliver, Win. Much overdue. I do not want to interrupt your work, but I'd be obliged if you'd permit me to unburden myself of a confession. And you might be interested by the tale, such as it is."

"Tell on, Joe," Mr. Winslow said briskly. "Won't stop me painting on a day like this! And the story may entertain the young lady better than my sparse chat."

It was true that Mr. Winslow did not talk much while he was making a picture. Aurelia had counted the stones in the wall enough times already that she was relieved to listen to anything, even a stranger's plaint.

"I am afraid it is not a happy story — it goes back to the war."

"Everything does," Mr. Winslow murmured in a gentle voice.

"I had a friend, Moylan. Friend of my brother's wife's brother, to begin with — met him in '63. You remember when my brother Sam got caught in the Battle at Gettysburg — killed instantly. I know that was a mercy, though it's still hard to accept. Well. Moylan was at the memorial service back in Curwensville, and I met him there.

"Then, in '65, my troop and I were in Georgia — terrible times; stinkin' bad. One major told us — I remember him, word for word, but we were just so tired at the time, we just stared at him. He told us, 'Take everything the damned Rebs —' Excuse me, miss, I'm quoting. 'Take everything the Rebs have been hoarding, right down to the damned red dirt in their gardens. And then, burn the dirt.' And we did it! By that time, we just wanted it over: Georgia was hell, and we were stuck in red mud, following orders for all eternity."

Aurelia had never seen red dirt; she had only seen red brick and terra-cotta. She wondered if Corporal Grunreiter's major's orders had turned people's gardens into brick. She wondered briefly what blood looked like on red mud, but that was too horrible to think about. She caught onto Mr. Grunreiter's words again.

"I got a little cut up — no great thing. Then, one day, at

the infirmary, they bring in some men wounded at Resaca, and here comes Moylan, not so badly shot, but feverish. And he knew. You know, it seemed they mostly all knew, when they weren't going to make it. All around you, folks were always praying. And . . . he gives me a letter he'd been writing to his sweetheart, says, 'Joe, give this to Miss Kelly.' Told me where she was — he hadn't addressed it, yet. And then he squeezed my hand that had the letter in it. . . ."

He paused and Aurelia heard two heavy sighs, his and Mr. Winslow's. She grasped what had happened. The still June air, in that moment, seemed too mute. The visitor went on.

"That was in May. Then, in October, my brother Davy took one at Cedar Creek."

Cedar Creek, Aurelia thought, *the grown-ups keep talking about Cedar Creek*, and the hot afternoon washed around her like seawater. She leaned back, ever so slightly, against the stones. *Corporal Grunreiter's brother Davy, and Mrs. Farwell's husband*, she thought, *". . . in the dusk of eternity meet."*

Mr. Grunreiter was saying now that he had tried to find Miss Kelly after the war, but it was apparently a common name in some New England towns, and his family responsibilities, now that his brothers were gone, had intervened before he could succeed. Then he had been offered an opportunity to go to Munich, Germany, to take a position where he would learn the newest etching techniques. The money was good and the work exciting, and for these many years, he had been living with cousins in Bavaria. Now he had come home to America, though, hoping to fulfill his friend's sacred trust.

"But I shall not tell any more now. You *are* painting slower than when I walked over."

Mr. Winslow did not demur.

"When you come back, Joe, we'll have better weather for the bass," he promised.

"Better for us than them," Mr. Grunreiter agreed as he stood to go back to the house. "Now, if I'm catching that train, I'd better go get packed, and redd up Mrs. Homer's guest room before I absquatulate."

Mr. Homer saw the look on Aurelia's face.

"Means 'leave,'" he explained, anticipating a question. "I expect it's a military term. Hold still, now. Just a little longer . . ."

"There, now. There." Mr. Winslow let out a deep breath. "Done. At ease, miss."

Aurelia dropped the basket and bent over, stretching toward her pinched toes.

"Is your friend from Philadelphia?" she asked when she straightened up. She wished she'd had the nerve to speak up while Mr. Grunreiter was still there. Living in Germany, he probably hadn't even heard of the *Aspiration* — but somehow, it was the principle that mattered.

"I beg your pardon?" Mr. Winslow said. Clearly, he was

still so immersed in thinking about his watercolor painting, her question had not sunk in.

"He said 'redd up.' I am told that people from Pennsylvania say that. Is he?"

"Oh, I see. Yes, he was with the Sixth Pennsylvania Cavalry. But not Philadelphia — out in the Alleghenies, I believe. He might have worked out of Philadelphia."

"Because I might be from Philadelphia." Aurelia was surprised at the words as they slipped out. Even though it was only "might be," saying it aloud was like touching the good-luck flowers on her blue trunk.

"Might be?" Mr. Winslow had propped the painting up on the wall. Aurelia could see now why he liked her dress: It was the same color as the lichened gray wall, the same color as the shadows under the clusters of cloud.

"And another thing: I am not Miss Ellicott." She felt she couldn't stop herself. "I am Miss Sandborn, remember? I only work for Miss Ellicott."

Mr. Winslow's head swiveled from the watercolor, and he looked into Aurelia's accusing eyes. He looked stricken.

"I *beg* your pardon, Miss Sandborn. Of course. Miss Sandborn. Forgive me. I meant no disrespect to your family."

"It's not my family's name. I mean — I don't remember my family's name."

"And you might be from? . . . My dear girl!" Mr. Winslow seemed profoundly confused.

Aurelia immediately felt ashamed of her bluntness. He had not intended to hurt her feelings. He had no idea that her life was more complicated than what showed. Perhaps she should explain? Mr. E. Hancock hadn't come after her so far. What harm would it do, to tell someone? Mrs. Prentice had always told her not to feel embarrassed about her childhood. Why not tell Mr. Winslow? He did not seem the sort of person who would lose a key, once you trusted him with it.

"I was shipwrecked," she began. She had not said the words in years. "And the ship was from Philadelphia. I was very young — I don't remember much about it. They said my mother wrapped me up in a quilt and an oilcloth cloak. My mother . . ." She stopped talking. Mr. Winslow did not speak. When she could look him in the eye again without tears threatening, she went on. "I remember my mother, but I don't remember my last name. I only remember seeing Mr. Sanborn, from Gloucester, leaning over to pick me up, and seeing the scar on his cheek. I was cold, and he was so . . . tender, and so concerned. And I was named for him, because he rescued me. But he's not my family. He never came to visit me while I was growing up."

Mr. Winslow was looking thunderstruck.

"You're Sanborn's foundling! Well, I'll be!" And then, a look of even greater astonishment washed over his face. "I've seen your quilt."

Thus it came out, that Mr. Winslow had lived in Gloucester a few years ago, himself, and had known the librarian.

"A very handsome quilt — squares, light blue and blue-green and black, and touches of zinnia red. He had it over the back of a rocking chair in his office. He told me about finding you! Quite a story! My dear girl! So, you're Sanborn's little angel! But, you know, he did visit you. He only stopped because . . . er . . ." Mr. Winslow stammered to a halt. "Well. People were saying . . . because they named you for him. . . . The thing was, there was no unaccounted-for child on the passenger list. And — oh, I remember this story very well — they did not recover all the passengers' bodies, so they were not sure of the actual identity of the woman. I remember him saying, of the charity ladies insisting on giving him your quilt, 'That's my Scarlet Letter.' Poor man, his wife wouldn't let him bring it home!"

"The ship was not taking us home — oh!" Aurelia turned away from Mr. Winslow for a moment, staring off across the yard and realizing. "I didn't know I knew that. We were going to . . . to *Grandmère's.*" Suddenly, she was crying.

Mr. Winslow put a hand on her shoulder and patted awkwardly a few times, then just held it in a firm clasp for a moment.

"Memories are treasures and torments," he reflected in a sad, strained voice. After a few seconds, he roused himself and added, "And so tricky. You have this one particular memory that is so precious — yet it's inaccurate. Sanborn has no scar."

Aurelia stopped sobbing as he handed her a pristine, folded handkerchief.

"Yes, he does. On his left cheek. I *do* remember his face! I do!"

"It must have been a trick of the light. Or a shadow."

He paid her another silver dollar.

She kept his handkerchief until she could wash and press it for him. The pinafore needed doing up, too, being smudged by this time with more earth, moss, and charcoal than cloud shadows.

Miss Mattie came out and told them there would soon be a new addition to the Homer homestead, in the form of a smooth bicycle track, which would not have log wagons heaving along, digging up the road surface every time one went for a spin.

Miss Calantha showed Aurelia some old issues of *Harper's Weekly* in which Mr. Winslow's drawings of the soldiers appeared. Since Aurelia had not seen Grunreiter's face, she could not recognize which of the men in the pictures was him.

And, again, Wayland was not there. But, while Aurelia was waiting to renew *Uarda*, Elima came in with Sarah Meadows and Sarah's brother, Tom. Aurelia tried to be invisible, but, standing at the librarian's desk, she could not succeed.

"Aurelia Sandborn, you do know Mr. Meadows, do you not?" Elima said, sweet as pie.

"Oh, sure," Thomas answered for her. "We see each other all the time at school."

Aurelia acknowledged them with a smile and a nod. They were being rather loud for the library, she thought. Three gentlemen were on the premises at the moment, attempting to read the papers.

"You'll never guess what I made him tell me," Elima gushed. (And that *was* one thing Elima did do from time to time. . . .) "Your friend, Mr. You-know-whom-I-mean was not with the young troubadours on a certain night not long ago. And here I was, assuming it must be he! But it was not. It was — Thomas!"

Aurelia had not thought it was Wayland who led "The Sands o' Dee." She was quite certain he had understood her request about no more shipwrecks, no more woe.

"It *was* for Mary," Sarah said. "Right, Tom?"

The mild and angular Thomas bobbed his head up and down and he scowled at his sister.

"And next time, it won't be 'Sally in Our Alley,' it'll be 'The Erie Canal,' and see how you like everyone talking about that, sis," he muttered. "But, yes. Anyway, Mary wasn't pleased, after all, and now she's off me."

"Oh, she will dance with you at the cotillion, I think," Elima consoled him.

"Wish you didn't have to be in an upper class to come to the dance," Tom said earnestly to Aurelia. "I'd like to put my name on your dance card."

"That is kindly said," Aurelia said quietly. "But I'm afraid cotillion gowns are not within the budget of one who is saving for her own education beyond high school. It is probably better for me to continue in my simpler amusements."

"I wonder with whom Mr. The-one-I-meant-before *will* dance?" Elima said innocently. "Oh! And the *most* delicious story! You will be entertained by this bit a little bird told me. Twitch had her pa call on your artist to line him up a commission to paint her in her cotillion rig, which is shell pink *peau de soie* and makes her look like a big, old, blowsy peony — doesn't it, Sally?"

"Oh, Elima, you are wicked," Sarah scolded, laughing. Two of the gentlemen reading turned to look at her.

"That's not the richest part," Elima went on, whispering. "Mr. Homer scarcely spoke to Mr. Twitchell, once he knew what he came for. Then he sent 'round a note that said, 'Life is too short, and oils dry too slowly, for me to paint any ideas but my own. I regret, I must decline the opportunity you offer.' Livia was fit to be tied! Amity and I had a good chuckle at her expense, I admit."

☆　　☆　　☆

"I declare, she is exactly like her mother, that one," Miss Calantha said privately to Aurelia after the others had departed. "And there never was a bigger Mrs. Mind-our-business than Beulah Worthy — a very good-hearted soul, but a busybody. Well. Some are born to gossip, others have gossip thrust upon them. Don't let it bother you, Aurelia. People make foolish decisions when they worry too much about what other people think."

Chapter 12

Through June, Mr. Winslow Homer worked on the oil painting on nineteen sunny afternoons. He paid Aurelia nineteen dollars. She grew familiar with the scents of turpentine and linseed oil. Union sat on the grass in the shade, being Mr. Winslow's brush holder, for which he was paid a total of five dollars. The brush holder was also the lemonade pourer, hornet chaser-offer, factotum, and general errand boy between Mr. Winslow and the rest of the world he did not want pestering while he painted.

Aurelia missed Wayland. She was rather ashamed of how sorely she missed him, for she missed him even more than she missed Mrs. Prentice, who sent her two brief notes, but not a real letter yet (though surely she would). Reluctantly, she saw that it had been a most unusual set of circumstances that had thrown Wayland and her into each other's company so often in May. She was not sure, now, when he found time for the library, or when he would find time for her.

She attempted to write a poem about this melancholy thought. It was a melancholy poem. She put it in her blue trunk and did not show it to anyone. She could *never* be so brave about telling her private feelings. Could she?

Once a week, or so, Wayland was at the Homers', visiting with his uncle. When he had the Harvard bicycle with him, he always came to fetch Union for a practice ride. Union was getting better, but he was not yet secure enough about tipping over to invite his mother or father to watch him. One day when Wayland came over, Aurelia was in the middle of her sitting with Mr. Winslow. Wayland saw them, though he did not interrupt. Another time, she was hanging out laundry, and they talked briefly.

"I am working the morning shift at Fussburton's with my father. I fix the trimmers when they jam, jobs of that sort. I'm the lad with the oil can." Indeed, she had noticed a difference in the dapples on his hands. He offered her one of the two ripe early peaches in the sack he'd brought from Howe's. She stopped work for a few moments to eat the juicy fruit. "Then, weekends, I'm at Mr. Knight's, helping the farrier. No time for writing poems, but you'll see, Aurelia. I *will* get *one* year at Harvard, and see what comes of it. If I do well, perhaps I can apply for a scholarship. I am sorry I don't have more time to visit these days."

Aurelia was glad he had said it.

Mr. Winslow had become moody. Aurelia thought perhaps he had been embarrassed by the personal nature of their conversation about her past. But mostly, he was simply not very talkative. Perhaps he did not wish to encourage Union, who occasionally talked to himself or hummed a bit as he drew a cartoon of his own. Mr. Homer also sometimes hummed. (Aurelia hummed when she was sweeping up after breakfast, but she did not hum while Mr. Homer was painting.)

One day, Mrs. Mattie came out with a dewy, green-glass pitcher of switchel.

"Your mother is going up to the Willows, without your father underfoot, to get them settled in for the summer up there. He will be here for the Fourth," she told him.

"The Old Man is like the bad penny," Mr. Winslow acknowledged. "He always does show up again." He did not sound irritated, though perhaps he sounded resigned. When she had gone back to the house, he made the first personal remark to Aurelia that he had, for days. "When the gold rush was on, he sailed off around the Horn," he said almost casually, as if he were Mark Twain spinning a campfire yarn. "I was your age, Union. And it was as if he'd sailed off the end of the earth."

Aurelia had a sudden inkling of comprehension, what it would be like for Union to lose the father he knew. Mr. Winslow continued.

"But he came back. He came back from California — and everything was whole again. He was a perfect Ulysses, back from Troy — lots of stories and no money for his trouble, but that was not so hard. Some fathers *don't* come back, though you hope and hope, and that *is* hard. The day does not dawn, the sun does not rise, that I do not notice that mine *does*."

Day by day, the painting came into focus. Mr. Winslow worked his brushes as if they were magic wands. He did not smile while he was painting. Sometimes, Aurelia thought, he looked terribly sad. Sometimes, he would put down his brush and pace back and forth, just looking at her and . . . well, not scowling. But looking terribly sad.

"Wish Harrigan would come 'round with the Harvard," Union mused grumpily one day. "It's dull here."

"No offense taken," Mr. Winslow said sharply. A moment later, he put down his brush. He stood up and paced a bit, muttering, "Dull here, eh. Comes down to that. Well, live and learn. You're not the first to say that about . . . the way I do things." He took a long sip from his lemonade.

"How did *you* learn to paint?" Aurelia asked him, glaring at Union.

Mr. Winslow was lighting his pipe. Aurelia could tell he was exasperated — he rarely wasted prime-light time on filling, tamping, and smoking during a session, and he did not paint with his pipe in his mouth.

"My mother taught me," he said. "She is a horticultural expert. Mattie has an album of her pictures of flowers you would enjoy looking at — remind me, when we are done today." He fidgeted with his palette, squeezing out a dab of carmine and gingerly smearing it into one side of the Chinese white. "Best rule she taught me, one of her rules for achieving vibrancy — something my mother is very good at — always include some element of red. Red is necessary to enliven all the other tints in a composition."

Mr. Winslow saw that his smoke was drifting toward Aurelia, and he waved a sheet of sketch paper to dispel the cloud. She wasn't sure if he was speaking for her benefit or Union's.

"I was a boy, of course, and most of my drawings were of ships — flags were a good place to put in some red. Battle scenes, bear hunts — such grim things, some of them, but all of them bold, what a boy draws! And with so much black — for boys always enjoy those good, hearty black blots and strong lines — one puts in a lot of red to make it exciting. They seem to balance each other, red and black, black and red. Like cards. All your fortune seems to be in those cards."

He stopped for a moment, and Aurelia had a feeling he was saying out loud things he'd meant to say to someone else and had not found a chance to get said.

"Well. Mother's watercolors notwithstanding, that is pretty much where I was in my work at *Harper's*." He waved a hand, a dismissive gesture. "But the flags and splotches from my boyhood turned into . . . real blood, ruined men. Friends cut down all around while one is trying to save oneself from disaster, even if one . . . cannot save them. War is not all black and red, not by a long shot; but the red's far too much, and in all the wrong places. I was truly sick of it, after the war. And I realized: In fact, black does not balance red. It charges it. Green is what it takes to balance red." He said it, Aurelia thought, as if he were talking about more than colors. He said it as if it were a realization that had once knocked him off his horse.

"About that time, I became acquainted with a young lady with red hair. Lighter than mine — than it used to be. Hers is what they call Titian, golden red. Not a stylish color, admittedly, though she was a girl who wanted to be stylish and asked me to paint her as a dark-haired Gypsy, and as a blonde, and as anything but what she was. Until — one day. One day, one spring day, she was wearing her favorite wrapper, which was of scarlet plush. Big buttons down the front — really quite lovely. She was reading a new book she'd started — she was quite a reader. *A Dog of Flanders*, I think it was."

He caught Aurelia's eye just then and did not look away briskly as he usually did.

"Nothing on earth," he said deliberately, "will ever be as beautiful as she was, that day. It wasn't that *she* smiled on me — though, that day, she did. It was nature smiling on us both. I do believe that. A moment of eternity that will not come again. I shall never paint like that again."

The sad look came back to the face that had been transfigured for the moment. Aurelia realized she knew what happened next. *Clare Skye is lost.*

"We had a falling out. The critics didn't like that picture, for one thing — didn't like the green shading I used to balance the scarlet — so much scarlet, and none of it blood or flags! In fact, it was almost red-orange. How could that be a manly piece of work! I'd painted clover, and they thought that was Fenian, or some such nonsense. At any rate, *she* took offense. She preferred a more private mode of . . . well. I cannot paint her anymore. However beautiful, she is no longer available as a subject for my art. That is that. That was the touch of red in my life, and it is now consigned to my memory."

Aurelia thought of the afternoon she and Wayland gathered laurel, of the sunlight on Wayland's hair when he came riding up the drive, capless. She wondered when they would be able to spend such an afternoon together again — *if* they ever would.

Mr. Winslow shrugged and put down his pipe. He took a long sip from his lemonade, went back to his easel, and began to daub his brush into the pale pink paint to address the details of the laurel flowers.

"I continue to do my work," he murmured, "though it's not the same. How can it be? But I shall look for the touch of red, here and there, wherever, in whatever I am painting."

"You know what *my* old man would say," Union said to Aurelia later. " 'Let's tie the white ribbon around that conversation, shall we?' "

At dawn's earliest light on the Fourth of July, the veterans fired the cannon on the Common, and boys and girls ran outside with tin horns tooting. The bell in the Baptist Church steeple tolled thirteen times, once for each of the Revolutionary colonies that became the first United States. At seven o'clock in the morning, a lad galloped around town in imitation of Paul Revere, yelling to warn Townsendites that the redcoats were on their way to seize the armory at Concord. Aurelia thought of Mrs. Sinclair's teapot. Union and his chums lit firecrackers and hurled them into the middle of Main Street (when, perhaps, it would have been better to wait a moment or two longer after Mr. Gleason's somber carriage had driven past). (Not the hearse, as Union pointed out, soon thereafter, to his father.)

One year ago, Aurelia thought. She had met Wayland one year ago, today: talking about books, fetching firecrackers. Did Wayland realize this was a sort of anniversary? Or was she the only one on earth who would give a thought to it?

Two o'clock found many of the town's young people gathered at the Big Eddy of the Squannicook, enjoying an impromptu picnic of peanuts and gingerbread. There was a general gathering planned at the Homers' house at dusk, when the fireflies would come out, and the fireworks would commence.

Some of the fellows — and Wayland was among their number — had removed their footwear and were wading along the edge of the water. Aurelia longed to join them, but the young ladies had spread their shawls to sit on, by the sandy side of the water, or over the two big tree trunks that had come to rest there. Several were much involved in determining whether the direction of the sun and density of the summer foliage required the use of parasols.

"Come, girls," Sarah Meadows called. "Instead of lopping around, let's get up a game the lads will enjoy as much as we do — a round of Philopenas!"

Aurelia had never played the game before. It seemed risky, as it involved being questioned. Yet there was no denying everyone's eagerness for such revelations as were to come; so the fellows were commanded to attend the quickly convened court of justice, all present arranged themselves in a circle, and the first three judges were assigned to the bench — Sarah, and the two girls to her right. The accused, opposite them across the circle, was Fred Wagner, Amity's false sweetheart.

"First question," Sarah declared. "Who is the prettiest lady present?"

"My sister, Alice," Fred replied — an answer not to be challenged, Aurelia saw.

"What would you say," the second judge charged, "if you woke up and found yourself living your heart's desire?"

"Please, pass me that third turkey drumstick," Fred replied with a laugh.

"You wicked miscreant!" Sarah scolded him. "We cannot prove it a perjury, but mind yourself! Third question: Which lady makes the most cutting remarks?"

"That would be — Miss Worthy," the hapless Fred replied.

The judges conferred briefly, and then hammered on a tin lunch pail, with a shoe for a gavel.

"We find you guilty of base fibbing. Livia makes the most cutting remarks, for she bought new embroidery scissors from you, after trying out every size in the store, right up to hedge shears."

Aurelia was astonished at how fast gossip traveled.

"So Fred owes a token of his repentance to — Elima. Next case!" Sarah decreed.

The next three judges included Livia. The accused was Laurence Boutelle.

"Who is the prettiest lady here?" the first judge asked, for she was not an original thinker, but she was entirely practical.

"Miss Ellicott," Laurence declared promptly.

"And who, the cruelest?" was the next required of him.

"Miss Ellicott," was the quiet answer.

"And did you bring her flowers not long ago?" Livia commanded him to say.

"I have never presumed she would accept a gift from my hand," was Laurence's passionate reply.

The judges conferred, and then the tin pail clanged for order in the court.

"We find the defendant not guilty. But we say, Miss Ellicott has to repent and pay a philopena to *him*, by moonrise tonight. Mr. Laurence, on your honor, you must report to us when you've been duly paid. Next case!"

Next, moving to the right around the circle, were Cornelius, Elima, and Thomas. Across from them was Aurelia. This time, the judges conferred before asking. Aurelia desperately hoped they would not ask about Boston. To her astonishment, they did not.

"Who spends the most time admiring A. S.?" Tom asked hopefully, adding, "You have to tell the truth, now."

Aurelia was rather nettled by that last remark.

"I always do tell the truth, Mr. Meadows," she said staunchly. "And the truth is, no one admires me more than Uncle Adams, Miss Ellicott's dog."

"My brother's dog," Amity amended. "And it's true. He especially admires her when . . . when there's *liver* for supper."

Titters went around the circle.

"Overruled," Cornelius said. "Tom should have said, What person? The truthful answer is W. H. So you must pay W. H. a philopena before moonrise, Miss Sandborn."

"And we shall be watching for him to report it to us," Elima added meaningfully.

As she had failed the very first question, Aurelia's turn passed. When she was no longer under scrutiny, Aurelia looked over at Wayland, hoping to catch his eye. She hoped the game had not cost him embarrassment, hoped he was not ashamed to be teased about her. He was standing next to Laurence, who was saying something close to his ear. Wayland was gazing away across the river to the chokecherry trees on the other side. He did not see her, or did not want to.

The game broke up after three more were tried, Wayland not among them.

Father Homer distributed quarters to all the youthful patriots, and Mr. Howe opened his store to their demand for gunpowder in the most colorful varieties. Aurelia closed Uncle Adams into the screen porch, where, she knew, the poor little beast would bury his head in the cushions of the rattan settee until the night's torpedoes were done exploding. Wayland found her there.

"Miss Not-really-a-Alcott," he said, looking right at her, not away at the trees, or off at his own ideas. "May I escort you to Howe's to purchase a supply of the 'rocket's red glare'? You do owe me a philopena before moonrise."

"And if I walk down the block with you, you'll consider it paid?" she asked, although she had in mind something else entirely that she'd been waiting to suggest.

"We shall discuss it. Meanwhile, I think I may need a Roman candle or two."

First she ran upstairs, to the slide-top box.

"Here," she said when she came back. She handed him seven silver dollars.

"Whoa!" he said. "This isn't a little philopena."

"Isn't meant to be. It's your share of what's come from Sandborn, Harrigan, and Ellicott. It's further laurel profits. Union also gets his share."

"'Relia, I can't accept this," Wayland protested gently. "You and Union have been working for Mr. Homer ever since the garlands. Besides, what about when Mr. Homer is done with the painting? You will still need to earn your keep."

"Mrs. Mattie is going to pay me the same rate to sew for her in my spare time. Mrs. Ellicott said I may. And I shall not split *that* money with anyone! But you agreed, about the laurel," she went on anxiously, for she had thought this through for weeks, and was quite sure she had a good plan. "Union wants his bicycle soon. I can't go to college for years, in any event; not until I'm done with high school. Now, you know this modern school committee doesn't want Mrs. Farwell to bother with Latin anymore, but I have my heart set on it. Miss Calantha says she doesn't remember enough, but you could tutor me. That could be part of our partnership agreement. And I would be helping you to meet Mr. Emerson. If the court of justice had asked *you* your heart's desire, it would have been Harvard — isn't that true?"

She looked up earnestly into the handsome quandary that was his face, just then.

"Not entirely, Miss Sandborn," he said, with a fond, funny look that Aurelia rather liked.

"Well, you must take the spondulix — if only, so you'll be able to report to the judges that I have paid my debt; for I shan't give you anything else before moonrise."

"Hmm. We shall see about that, Miss Sandborn," Wayland said.

They went to purchase firecrackers.

If there was one thing a person shouldn't underestimate about Elima, Aurelia thought at the store, it was her curiosity. Very well. She should have something to occupy her this evening. Aurelia bought a red tin horn.

Over at the Homers', while Wayland was fetching her a piece of strawberry shortcake, Aurelia found Mr. Winslow and gave him the horn.

"A touch of red for today, sir," she said.

"And I thank you for it," he said, bowing most graciously.

"Now," Aurelia told him, "if you would be so kind — you must go over to Miss Worthy and tell her that my debt is paid. Will you do that for me, sir?"

Mr. Winslow gave her a sharp look. Then he raised the red tin horn to his mustache and gave it a try.

"This might be good for calling mallards, come autumn," he remarked. "The one with the pink parasol?" He tipped his boater to Aurelia and rose to do her bidding. Mr. Winslow was a perfect gentleman.

"Let's go sit on your wall," Wayland said when he'd brought the shortcake. They walked close together toward the old canal. Wayland smelled gingery, and a little of the river, and a little of Roman candles. "Tell me what you think about," he said, "standing there all summer."

"I think about summer. I think about standing," she said, suddenly shy.

"And? . . ."

"Um . . . flowers. And shadows. Clouds . . . history."

"When I am not with you," Wayland murmured, "sometimes I think about you. Do you think of me sometimes?"

They had reached the wall, and he balanced the two plates of strawberries on a flat stone. He put his hands gently on Aurelia's shoulders and turned her to face him. He was looking into her eyes. She nodded, wordless.

The first flowers of fire began to burst the sky with sound that echoed off the hills like distant battle. Fireflies were hovering in the dusk. Like new white flowers, they starred the laurel. In the shadows down by the gate in the stone wall, Wayland kissed her once. Just once.

Well, twice.

Chapter 13

While it may be true that not all first kisses are magical and full of sweetness, Aurelia was a happy girl the morning after Wayland's and hers. If anyone had asked the highly unlikely question, *Can something as simple as kissing someone just once (well, twice . . .) change the world?* she would have had to answer *yes*, or owe someone an enormous philopena. Whatever sorrow, fear, anger, or worry plagued the weary globe that day, Wayland wanted to draw closer to her. She knew this for certain, and she could hardly think of anything except her good luck and his kiss. (Well, kisses.)

And then — what had come over Miss Amity?

The fireworks seemed to have started something, for the furniture of her bed-sitting-room was migrating again. Aurelia saw that Amity had managed to put towels and hearth rugs under the feet of the bigger pieces, so sliding them wouldn't mar the floor; where she could, she had rolled back the carpet.

"Think we can move this big wardrobe without emptying it?" Amity asked her.

Aurelia gave it a push, and it didn't move; but when Amity pulled the hearth rug and Aurelia resumed pushing, they managed to slide it to the only space on the wall where Amity hadn't yet tried it.

"Who really left that bouquet?" Amity asked casually. "Because — I went for a long walk with Laurence, as payment of my philopena, and we had an *entirely* pleasant time. Did you know he plans to study architecture? He is going to Amherst in September. But he still maintains it was not he who left the nosegay. Was it you, Aurelia? You knew about Livia and Fred betraying me, didn't you?"

It took Aurelia a moment to sort through what Amity was saying — accusing her of? Admitting? Amity did not seem to be angry. If anything, she seemed cheerful.

"I saw them together," Aurelia confessed. "I didn't know what to say. Livia hadn't much to say to Fred until his father started to talk of the new bank; then she suddenly discovered he was her *beau idéal*, after all. Do you mind awfully?"

"Not really, I find. Laurence is so much kinder, and more fun." She thought a moment, then added, "More than Fred *and* more than Livia."

"You know how many times he sent his regards," Aurelia reminded her.

"I know, and — Aurelia, I know I have been lazy and horrid toward you. I freely own it, and now I beg your pardon. I was already ashamed in my heart, I reckon, but Livia is hard to argue with. Yet it is so wonderful, how Laurence has opened my eyes, with his patient, loyal interest! I should like to be as good as he thinks me."

Amity made a funny face when she said this, and Aurelia was glad of it. This new Amity was refreshing, but Aurelia suspected such a confiding mood would not last — it was not Amity's usual character. Still, it was touching to hear her open her heart, and Aurelia admired her for it. She thought, for the thousandth time, how glad she would be when she no longer had to keep her own past secret.

"It is not as if I don't know," Amity admitted, "that I've had it all my own way with Papa and Mama, for the croup killed my poor little sister before I was born, and they loved her more than anything. Papa treats me as if I'm blown glass, and I have taken advantage of it — I see now how wrong I was. But I did think you were the one who left the flowers that so kindly soothed my hurt pride. I will not say, my broken heart, for I find it's not broken a bit. If you did not leave the posy, who did?"

"Union saw Livia in the store. I expect he did it."

"Union! Why, I thought he'd sworn himself my rival and enemy in all things!"

"Perhaps," Aurelia considered. "But, I think, not this year.

He *is* almost thirteen. He misses you, now you are too grown-up to share his quests and capers."

While they spoke, they had repositioned the old Hadley chest in the east light.

"The flowers on your trunk are carved," Aurelia commented. "The ones on mine are painted. They're good-luck flowers." She was thinking of her locket, which always used to be within the trunk, like its heart. She missed the faces of the man and the old-fashioned lady. How could Mr. E. Hancock be so cruel?

"The ones on mine are sunflowers," Amity was saying, fondly running her hand over the timeworn wood. "I think they are why I want to learn to make furniture — and I don't mean needlework cushions! Dovetails and rabbits and bird's-eye maple for me."

"I didn't know you cherish such a dream," Aurelia admitted.

"Probably not," Amity said with a shrug. "It drives Papa mad when I speak of it, for he thinks saws and splinters a bad mix with petticoats and trailing lace."

"Amity, have you seen Mrs. Mattie's trousers? There's no trailing . . ."

But Amity had already opened the Hadley chest and was holding up an envelope postmarked New York, with a return address on Broadway.

"Sewing is not my favorite thing to do," Amity said. "But

I sent away for a pattern, and if you'll make us each a pair, I shall make Papa let us wear them."

There were fourteen more days of posing, fourteen dollars more remuneration.

As the shadows in the painting came into focus, she could see that, without the white stockings, she would have looked to be hovering above an abyss.

Blackberries and raspberries ripened. It was difficult to keep a pinafore white.

In the painting, except for the pink of the flowers, there was no touch of red.

She finally had a letter from Mrs. Prentice. There were two pages of merry stories about Kate and Jonathan and baby Tim, and then, on a separate sheet, the part Aurelia had been most anxious to read.

> *Miss Mills told me about your visit to her when you left the S's. She was much moved by the care you took to ask her to send someone over that very afternoon to the S's to take over caring for the Mrs. They found the type of individual you suggested, experienced and able to fend for herself. E. H. was not, she thinks, entirely keen on the new arrangement, but he was too lazy to resist Miss Mills's helpfulness. My dear, you were right to leave. E. H. was always mean to you, and I was grown too used to his weak character to expect*

any better or worse of him. I am sorry to have left you in such straits.

Kate and Jonathan are planning a stay up at Prout's Neck, Maine, in August, and I shall be going along. I have arranged it with E. H. — I am to bring Mrs. S. with us (not him! He does not know I know your whereabouts). I will see to it we get her up to snuff. Sea air is good for that. Perhaps I shall be able to make a side trip to visit your new establishment in West Townsend. . . .

That news had been worth the wait!

Aurelia had a nightmare about a cupboard full of blue-and-white china falling on her. She awoke, yelling. Others awoke. They went back to bed. She went back to sleep.

Then she had a nightmare about seagulls speaking to one another. At first, they were frightening, then not so bad. She awoke realizing she missed the seagulls she used to see in Boston, but unable to remember what the gulls in her dream had been telling her.

She did not like the face in Mr. Winslow's painting, these days.

"It looks too much like me," she said to Mr. Winslow.

"Not you, too," he said. "I will not render you as golden-haired. I will not make your hands or feet smaller, or your nose less pink."

"Well, just keep that shadow where it is, please."

"Only your chin shows, anyway," Union pointed out helpfully. "If you don't like it, grow a beard."

Wayland was still working his two jobs, and Aurelia still did not see him very often. One afternoon, Wayland started to joke that they were "like ships passing in the night," but Aurelia asked him not to say that. She had decided she wanted to tell him everything she'd told Mr. Winslow about the *Aspiration*, for the telling had been a huge relief — at last, her past woes had forged a connection with someone else's life, instead of keeping her apart. There hadn't yet been any occasion when she and Wayland were alone together long enough, but she had started to feel a great yearning to explain herself to him by explaining her losses. It felt different, knowing he wanted to be with her; but she'd discovered a new worry, for she already cared for him so, she didn't know what she would do if she ever lost him.

Besides, she wanted him to kiss her again.

Mr. Winslow's friend Grunreiter came back from his errand without having had any further success. He and Mr. Winslow went out fishing every morning, rain or shine; on fine days, he was to be seen napping in the hammock under the elms while Mr. Winslow painted. Actually, as July streamed past, Mr. Winslow spent far more time fishing than painting. Aurelia spent far more time sewing Amity's blue bloomers than she spent polishing the silver for Mrs. Ellicott, but no one complained about the arrangement.

One afternoon near the end of the month, a delegation from the Townsend chapter of the Daughters of Martha came to call on Mrs. Ellicott. The delegation consisted of Mrs. Worthy, Miss Calantha, and Elima. Amity was curious and followed them all into the parlor. Mrs. Worthy asked that Aurelia be present.

When Aurelia heard that, she swallowed hard. A sickish feeling stirred within her.

"Pursuant to a telegram, we have received a letter from the Boston chapter," Mrs. Worthy began, her voice brimming with excitement. "Something has happened that has called the attention of certain generous benefactors of our endeavors to a circumstance of most exemplary nature, a splendid example of charity."

Aurelia seemed to feel the floor fly up beneath her. *The Boston chapter . . .*

Mr. E. Hancock had found her.

"REEF THE SKYSAILS!" Cicero roared.

Mrs. Worthy read the letter aloud.

The poor child no doubt felt obligated to repay my aunt for her considerable upkeep for so many years. We found it after she ran away. We feel she has probably been enticed by some blackguard into a perilous

[145]

extreme, and this thought is most painful to us. Yet, as the locket is her only inheritance from her own family, whoever they may have been — and it is regrettably true that they have never come inquiring after her, perhaps realizing she had landed in good circumstances and was better off where she was — of course, I must locate her and return it to her in person. *I will at that time, I assure you, recompense your noble organization for your pains. . . .*

"And the young woman who has inspired this singular devotion," Mrs. Worthy concluded, beaming, "is our Miss Aurelia Sandborn."

Everyone looked at Aurelia expectantly.

"It is true, then?" Mrs. Ellicott asked. She sounded baffled, almost hurt. "You ran away from the place, after they'd taken you in for all those years?"

"What is this about?" Miss Calantha asked in a firm, crisp voice.

"DON'T LET YOUR MOTHER HEAR YOU!" Cicero croaked.

"I won't see him," Aurelia stated, her voice stony. "Even to get my locket back."

Aurelia thought she could explain a bit of it. Just, that she did not mean to leave her locket. Just, that Mr. E. Hancock was not so friendly as the letter sounded.

But when she tried to say that much and no more, she began to cry. And once she began to cry, the world turned into a sea of bitter salt.

"Mrs. Prentice had to go take care of her daughter," she sobbed. "And I had to take care of Mrs. Sinclair, but I left her. Please, don't make me go back to Mr. E. Hancock. He . . . wanted me to come to his room at night and eat oysters and drink wine punch. He kept . . . crowding up against me so I couldn't get away. He stole my mama's locket, with the pictures in it."

Mrs. Ellicott had pulled Aurelia down to sit beside her the instant she began to weep, had thrown protective arms around her just as if she were her own child. Amity and Elima knelt by the sofa, each holding and stroking one of Aurelia's hands. Miss Calantha and Mrs. Worthy looked on, tender and outraged, while Aurelia choked and stammered out the story of storm and salvation, charity, kindness, and betrayal.

"The cad!" Mrs. Worthy exclaimed when Aurelia's tears had subsided. "It seems his nature is to use people for his low purposes. Why, he was well on the way to using *me* scandalously! Using the Daughters of Martha! All, to get you back . . . oh, it is reprehensible!"

"Amity, didn't I tell you it had to be something interesting?" Elima said. "I said, that Miss Sandborn has had some sort of interesting thing happen to *her*, I just know it. Don't you worry, Aurelia, he'll never lay a hand on you again. You have friends, and we won't stand for it."

"It is not merely that his behavior was so coarse," Miss Calantha said in a tone that made it clear what she thought of him. "But, in stealing your locket, he not only took something of quantifiable value; he also deprived you of your sole real clue to your family. That is unquantifiable cruelty."

"Yes," Mrs. Ellicott said. "Someone might have recognized the people in the portraits, if proper inquiries had ever been made."

"Beulah," Miss Calantha said, "when does he say he will arrive?"

"He says he is summering on Cape Cod and will be here in September."

"Oh, but we mustn't let him see Aurelia if she doesn't want him to!" Amity exclaimed. "It is too awful!"

"I shall take him into the Daughters' workroom and get him to show me the locket," Mrs. Worthy promised, with a look in her eye that was positively bloodthirsty. "And when he does, I shall bring out Judge Twitchell to give him what-for. That ought to send that whale oil salesman back to Boston pretty quick!"

"But we still won't really know about the ship and . . ." Miss Calantha's voice tapered into thoughtful silence.

"You should start attending when the Daughters meet," Elima said.

"Do you knit washcloths for the missions?" Aurelia asked. "I'm good at that."

"No, we sew cunning little blue flannel shirts for the orphans," Elima enthused. (It was one thing you had to get used to about Elima: She enthused a good deal.) "I mean," she amended, trying not to be tactless, "for the *little* orphans."

Aurelia grinned. "I'm good at that," she promised.

A half an hour later, the delegation had drunk their tea and were leaving, hugging Aurelia, patting her hand and promising that she had all their protection, and need not face Mr. E. Hancock Sinclair alone.

"But we really should try that experiment," Miss Calantha murmured to Aurelia. "Regarding the spirits."

Chapter 14

Miss Calantha was sure they ought to try it when the moon was full. Aurelia was to ask the spirit guides to allow her to speak with her mother. Wayland, informed in hushed whispers at the library, where he was perusing *Gulliver's Travels*, tended to be skeptical; but he admitted he'd like to speak with his mother, too, if it wouldn't be too much like hauling her out of the Good Place just when she'd settled in.

Then it occurred to Aurelia that Mr. Winslow's friend might want to ask the spirit guides how to find Miss Kelly.

"I shall invite him," Mr. Winslow assured her. "Might be just the thing to entertain him. We've already worked our way through pinochle, poker, and cribbage, but my father does not play. Shall I invite my father as well? He is singularly unafraid of ghosts."

It was already almost August, and any day, now, the Homer household would depart the neighborhood for a month at the shore. Aurelia was not sure why Mr. Homer still had her come over and stand under the bonnet every fair afternoon. Some days, his brush didn't seem to go near the girl in the painting. He would work the whole hour on the ferns in front of the brown rock, or the clouds where they layered in the upper sky, piled above their own shadows. He was not really looking at her, she thought. She did not mind — not even on the day when she realized he had pretty much painted away one of her feet. The merest glimmer of her left stocking was left.

The painting was almost done.

After some hesitation, Aurelia and Miss Calantha had decided to invite Mrs. Ellicott, Amity, and Elima to the séance.

"But you must not talk out of turn," Miss Calantha warned Elima. "It is not a frivolous endeavor. We want no chatter. It could spoil the experiment."

Elima nodded and uttered not a syllable.

Miss Calantha lived in a sixteen-sided white clapboard house of two stories, three porches, and a cupola with a widow's walk and a small glass conservatory room. All week, the heat had smothered the river wetlands, but by the evening of the séance, pewtery clouds were blustering down from the mountains, raising the wind, dropping the temperature by ten degrees in half an hour. The west windows of the Crofoots' parlor sporadically rattled in their sashes. Now and then even the heavy draperies billowed and fell as the company assembled early in the evening.

If Miss Calantha had not gathered all the delphiniums and poppies she could, to save them from the impending downpour, Aurelia thought, the parlor would have been forbidding, indeed. As it was, it was the most exotic place she could have imagined, for the clipper captain had decorated his home ashore with Japanese chairs carved with dragons, Korean bronzes, South Sea war canoe paddles, and Chinese porcelain. The vases where Miss Calantha had arranged the great armloads of flowers stood to either side of the fireplace and were taller than Aurelia. Each vase was wide toward the base, with a narrow neck and flared, piecrust-ruffle rim. Glazed from purest white to inky cobalt blue, their glimmering surfaces swirled with waves and fish scales, cranes and clouds, and Chinese sages in stiff gowns, who gazed mysteriously about their polished world. A good-sized ghost, it occurred to Aurelia, could fit into a genie bottle that big.

"What a quantity of . . . well, of things that could break," Aurelia murmured, awed. "I don't envy whoever dusts *this* room!"

"This room," Mrs. Ellicott informed her with a twinkle in her eye, "is precisely why I have no patience for dusting my own parlor. After doing this room to old Mrs. Crofoot's satisfaction for five years, I'd had enough."

"You were Miss Calantha's parlor maid?" Aurelia wondered if it were rude to sound amazed.

"Her mother's," Mrs. Ellicott replied. "A far worse trial."

In the center of the carpet stood a round ebony table set with lighted candles, an Egyptian stone incense burner topped with a sphinx, a bowl of water, and a large bar magnet. Chairs were set all around the table. Aurelia's was one of the ones with dragons.

Miss Calantha served them iced tea and ladyfingers while she explained the preparations she had made, and the procedure the madame of the Guides of the Inner Light prescribed. The youngest person present — Aurelia — was to wave the magnet over each person several times, right up their backs from waist to crown, being careful not to reverse the action — or the magnet — at any time. While she was doing this, everyone was to have their fingertips, previously immersed in the bowl of water, touching their neighbors' fingers. When Aurelia had finished with the magnet, she was to stand it in the center of the table, and take her own chair, dip her own fingertips, and touch those of the individuals on either side of her. Then, they would see what happened.

The candles flickered wildly until several people adjusted their chairs to block the draft. Aurelia began her circulation around the table. She waved the magnet behind Miss Calantha in long, smooth strokes, as if she were ironing. It was silly, wasn't it, trying to call ghosts? If ghosts would come when you called, people would always be calling on them — they'd never get to rest in peace. When she had magnetized Miss Calantha, Aurelia moved on around the table.

Thunder rumbled beyond Battery Hill. Ribbons of sandalwood fume twined up from between the sphinx's talons and dispersed into the gathering gloom. Would ghosts appear as vaporous forms, if they came? Would they look as they did before they died? Or as they did when . . .

Aurelia felt a momentary wave of light-headedness wash through her. The room was becoming eerie, especially when the lightning shadows fluttered around the hull of the staunch little house. She had reached Wayland. He had laid aside his jacket, for he'd been caught in the first gusts of rain, and his damp vest and shirt clung to him, defining the muscular curves of his back and shoulders. Aurelia supposed he needed a haircut, but she hoped he would not get one for another week. She liked standing close to him this way, inspecting him inch by inch. As she waved the magnet up his spine, she thought she could feel the magnet's effects in her own marrow. She wondered if the ghosts were feeling what she was feeling — surely, it would summon them, if anything could. She stood the magnet at the center of the table, took her place in the ebony dragon chair, wetted her fingers, and gave a hand each to Wayland and Miss Calantha.

They waited. The air seemed to crackle with invitation.

After a long moment of silence during which nothing of note transpired, Miss Calantha said, "Does everyone have their eyes closed?"

Father Homer stirred restlessly in his seat.

"The closure of the eyes is not likely to effect any significant difference in the flow of magnetic waves or cells of mind energies," he began.

"Everyone must have their eyes closed, I am sure," Miss Calantha said firmly. "We are here to listen, we are here to see the inner light. Please, dear spirits, tell us anything we ought to know."

Aurelia could feel how everyone's energy was tickling at their fingers. She could feel the warmth of Wayland's callused hand, and the sensitivity of Miss Calantha's paper-white touch. Their hands were in communion all around the circle, but nothing happened.

"God bless and save us," Father Homer intoned, "from any pernicious influences. We offer ourselves as vessels for prophecy and inspiration, and so on, and so forth. That is the point, is it not? When does your authority say the experiment will come to a boil?"

"In good time," Miss Calantha murmured. "Friendly spirits, we invite you, come among the mortals who cherish your memory. Or the memory of your memory."

"Ooh, I like that," Elima breathed.

But nothing happened.

"Perhaps, if we align our concentration," Father Homer encouraged. "Everybody say what spirits you're calling out to from this vale of tears. And we shall all concentrate with one another."

Miss Calantha nodded her approval, and then, realizing everyone still had their eyes closed in the candlelit room, she spoke.

"All right," she said. "I shall begin. I call my fiancé."

"I call my mother," Aurelia said when Miss Calantha squeezed her hand.

"I call my mother," Wayland echoed.

"My baby sister," Amity said. "Is that all right, Mama?"

"I call her, too," Mrs. Ellicott said.

"I call my brothers," Mr. Grunreiter said. "Perhaps they can see what I can't."

"I am content to see who turns up," Mr. Winslow said. "It is potentially a full house, already."

"I don't know anybody in particular who's dead," Elima said dreamily when it was her turn, "but I think it would be romantic if some spirit of a doomed lover came and asked us to do for it what it needs to be at rest. I read a most wonderful novel in which . . . well, I think it would be very interesting."

"I believe I should like to converse with the biblical Solomon," Father Homer decided. "If he's not doing anything more pressing."

Nothing happened.

"Perhaps, a few more words of remembrance," Miss Calantha suggested.

"My father always says," Wayland began in a low voice, as if he were musing out loud, "Mother was the making of us all. You'd get out of her way on cleaning days — she scrubbed like a madwoman. And she baked soda bread every day and yeast bread twice a week, I remember that. We kept a cow then, and John Patrick and Seamus churned the butter on Saturday evening, so Mother could play her fiddle for us. And she'd dance with Marianna and Bridey and Matthew and me while she was playing it. So, Mother, I believe you're in the Land of the Ever Young these days, but if you can sail a boat close to our mortal shore, you'd make your boy happy another time. But don't be troubling your sweet self. As you said, there's nothing I need that I can't get for myself if I work hard and love my books."

Aurelia felt her heart fill with his words.

After a moment's silence, Mrs. Ellicott cleared her throat.

"Elise was a good little girl, *jolie*, as pretty as Amity, but with hazel eyes and lighter hair, more like Union's. She was contrary when she was a year and a half old, but by two, she liked to be obedient. She always came when her mama called."

Aurelia thought of her mama; how she sprinkled sugar onto Aurelia's bread and milk, and how she scattered corn to the chickens in the yard and showed Aurelia how to find chickweed in the lawn and bring it back to the coop for them, and how to fool the hens into letting her hold a baby chick for a moment or two, but you had to be so, so gentle so they wouldn't be frightened. . . . If she told them all that, she thought, she would start crying; and what would that do to madame's magnetic channels?

She looked across the table at Mr. Grunreiter. He was in the other dragon chair, and the incense smoke around him looked as if it were the creature's breath. His eyes were cast down, but there was a look about his face — not frightening, exactly; more like, *haunted* — that gave her a chill at the nape of her neck.

"My two brothers both died in the war," Mr. Grunreiter said slowly, thoughtfully. "I turn my thoughts to them now. For years, now, I have been moving in a fog of loss, and I want to see my way through." He sighed heavily. "Win, forgive me. I haven't even told you the half of it. While I was abroad, tragic circumstance led to my brother's only child being given up for adoption, and despite the inquiries I've made every- where I thought I could find information, I have been unable to discover where my own closest flesh and blood lives now — or *if*. How could I let this happen? So it is having failed my family already that I seek their guidance. And hav- ing failed our friend's charge to me, I seek his help as well."

Aurelia felt another chill sweep over her. She could hardly take in the sense of what he was saying but found herself won- dering urgently what he would sound like without the German accent encrusting his words. Not that she didn't like his voice — she did — but there was something. . . . He said *my brother's only child.* . . .

"About my friend," Grunreiter added, "no one in Pepperell could tell me where to deliver his letter, or anything about Miss Kelly, who taught school there during the war."

Miss Calantha and Mrs. Ellicott gasped simultaneously.

"Miss *Callie*," Mrs. Ellicott corrected him.

"Was your friend's name *Julian*?" Miss Calantha asked in a voice that was quiet and firm and joyous.

"Yes! Julian Moylan!" Mr. Grunreiter exclaimed.

"Uncle Julian?" Wayland registered, immeasurably startled. "You knew my mother's brother? And *you* — were engaged to him?" He stared at Miss Calantha.

"Extraordinary," Father Homer expostulated. "We must glean some insights, eh?"

"Don't anyone, please, don't drop your hands — we must maintain our dynamic energy!" Miss Calantha implored, but her cheeks were red. "Julian called me Callie. I taught in Pepperell after I left off working at the Female Seminary when my mother passed on. My father opposed our marrying. That was when Julian enlisted. You . . . have a letter for me?" She raised a voice trembling with hope. "Oh, Julian, are you here now?"

A brilliant flash and crash of thunder shook the house.

"By Jove, that's some magnet!" Wayland muttered. "I feel like Franklin's key." Suddenly he smiled. "Actually, Uncle Julian made me my first kite, me and Matthew."

"Miss Sandborn, are you quite all right?" Mr. Winslow asked, for Aurelia was looking pale in the candlelight.

My brother's only child, she was thinking. *My brother's only . . . daughter. . . .*

Aurelia stared at Mr. Grunreiter, her heart suddenly hammering.

"Did you say 'Sandborn'?" asked Mr. Grunreiter, his attention swiveling sharply from Miss Calantha's excited tears.

"Aurelia?" Wayland's hand was quickly under her wrist to steady her.

"Aurelia? Aurelia Sandborn?" Grunreiter's voice was tense. "The Gloucester Sailors' Family Aid said *Boston* . . . but Sinclair said . . ."

The circle of hands *was* broken then, for Mr. Grunreiter slowly pushed his chair back, stood up, and circled the table to let himself down on his knees beside Aurelia's chair so that he was peering at her at her eye level. They gazed at each other, overwhelmed.

"Ach du liebe!" he breathed. "My child, my child! It *is* you! I am Uncle Joseph! You are not dead! You're here! Why did he tell me? . . . Let me look at you!"

"Uncle?" Aurelia tried, tentatively. Her mind was racing — she remembered . . . remembered. . . . "My uncle . . . Uncle Joseph, Uncle — oh, oh, Mama! Oh, Uncle!" A sob escaped her, as she reached out instinctively and stroked his dear, remembered face over and over, the saber-swiped flesh not quite hidden by his beard. "*Your* cheek! *Your* scar! Oh, how could I forget?"

"Davy!" Joe Grunreiter suddenly whooped. "Annabelle! I've found her!"

"My word!" Father Homer expounded. For once, he was not up to more comment.

"But there weren't any spirits," Elima said, disappointed. "The table did not move, and there was none of that tapping one hears of. Just because people have information for one another, that's not anyone returning from the dead — is it?"

Aurelia and Uncle Joseph were clasping each other's hands as if they could never let go, gazing at each other in rapt bliss and grief so mingled, they laughed and wept at once, and scarcely realized they were doing either.

"I *would* have known you, if not for your accent and the beard," Aurelia told him. "I remember your face, though I could recall only a child's names for everyone. You're *Uncle*! I thought it was Mr. Sanborn's face I always dreamed about."

"When you were little, after the war, when you and your mother and I all lived with *my* mother in Philadelphia, I kept it trimmed. I grew it out in Munich. But you! Your hair is like your mother's, but your features are like *my* mother's! I would have known this little Schlegel nose if I had once looked at *you*, instead of at Win's painting, with all his artistic shadows!"

"Ahem. Painting is not photography," Mr. Winslow protested mildly.

"Gracious Heaven," Father Homer proclaimed, "the infinite elegance of Thy creation and mercy leave us flabbergasted."

"If I am really Aurelia Grunreiter, though," Aurelia asked, "who is A. S.?"

"Your mother, Annabelle Shank, before she married my brother, Davy Grunreiter."

"And whose pictures were in my locket?"

A look of unbearable sweetness and loss came over Grunreiter's face.

"Her gold locket! She wore that every day, at home," he said softly. "Your mother, child, was an entirely lovable woman. Your father, Davy, of course, is one of the pictures. And she had painted the other, herself, of her own mother, when she was younger — Emilie Royer Shank. She visited us once; you called her '*Grandmère*.' Annabelle was — you are — of Arcadian French descent, as well as Bavarian."

"I knew it!" Mrs. Ellicott declared with satisfaction. "I knew it!"

"We were going to visit her," Aurelia said. "I only remembered that for the first time a few weeks ago. But — Shank was Mama's maiden name? As in, Daniel Shank, the captain of the *Aspiration*?"

"Annabelle's brother," Grunreiter explained.

"Dan Shank," Miss Calantha murmured. "Julian wrote me about him. I still have the letters. My dear Aurelia, to think, you're Danny Shank's niece. . . !" She shook her head in wonderment.

"Their father was from Lancaster County, Pennsylvania. He met your *grandmère* when she was at a girls' school near Albany. Daniel knew our older brother, Sam, first. Then he introduced your mother to Davy, to us all. After the war, the ones of us who were left had to pick up the pieces of our lives. Then my mother died, and my cousins in Bavaria invited me to come work for them. I had left for Europe, and Dan was taking you and Annabelle up to Petit Manan, Maine, to be with his wife and sons and the Royers up there, while I was away."

Aurelia drew in a sharp breath. "Then, you are not my only family left?" The idea was another happy shock.

"*Ach, mein Gott!* No, no, you are not the lonely survivor, *meine* Aura Lee."

"*Meine Aura Lee, mein Chickendee,*" Aurelia murmured, awash in floods of memory. "*We ride to the market for sugar and tea. . . .* You used to sing that to me! You all used to toss me on a blanket and sing, and we'd laugh and laugh!"

"We did, we did! You'd help my mother gather the eggs, and you loved the little chickies so — if only Davy could have seen you!"

"He never saw me?" Aurelia asked, suddenly hushed. No

wonder she had never recognized his photograph! She had never known her father, and he had never known her.

"We never knew if he'd even received Annabelle's letter telling him she was — He had leave a few months before he was shot."

"At Cedar Creek," Aurelia realized. "My father was a soldier."

"No, no — he was a chaplain. Picked off by a sharpshooter when he was standing with some officers. Davy was an abolitionist, but he would never have raised a weapon against another American. Or anyone else. He was a good shepherd, was what he was. He always said sinners were just children who had lessons still to learn — that as many sins stem from failures of education as from failures of character."

"Then — I do have a family religion?" Aurelia asked. What an astonishing thought!

Uncle Joseph laughed. "This is America," he assured her. "You may very well have three or four."

Miss Calantha did not read the whole of Julian Moylan's letter aloud, for much of it was the tender message of a lover still expecting to return, full of hopes and plans, endearments and daily concerns. What he'd written once wounded, though, betrayed a more somber expectation.

My dearest, I cannot say when I shall have leave to come to you and see my home again. . . . Here is the key of a safety box in the bank at St. Louis. In it are the proceeds of a long steamboat night of cards. I did not have opportunity to inform my executor, Hubbard. It is for my sister, Mary Ann, and her husband, Gerald Harrigan, and their children, and consists of nugget gold, three five-pound ingots same, a sack of coins, and some Nevada silver mining stock certificates (don't know what they are worth, but Yancey was pretty well fixed, and I did not win all he had, I can tell you that). . . ."

"Silver mining stock," mused Father Homer. "Someone may be very well off by this time — very well off, indeed."

Miss Calantha was weeping.

Wayland was cradling his hands around hers, which held the letter.

"My father called him names," she was murmuring. "He said Julian never really loved me, or he would have returned. I knew he loved me. I knew, if he lived, he would come home to me, sooner or later."

The storm rolled off down the river valley while they untangled the skeins of life story and sorted out the intricate ties that had brought them together. Eventually, however, her guests made their good-byes to Miss Calantha, leaving her to reread and grieve privately the love letter that had found her at last.

As they descended the front steps, a rim of coral-red glowed beneath the last trailing pennons of gray storm clouds. The street was strewn with windfallen branches, and they could see, up the way, the oak that had been struck and split by lightning.

"Miss Calantha has a copy of the same photograph of Uncle Julian that my mother had," Wayland remarked. "She thinks I look like him."

"Does Grandmère still look as Mama painted her?" Aurelia asked Uncle Joseph.

"When I saw her last fall, she seemed smaller than I remembered," he replied. "She has aged, of course. But your mama captured her likeness well in the miniature."

"I miss my locket," Aurelia admitted shyly. Uncle Joseph was holding her hand.

"A picture from nature of a loved one you can never again see," Mr. Winslow murmured. "A likeness of a loved one who has changed. Portraits of time's tide running."

"How lucky," Elima said, "that your mama could paint."

Chapter 15

The Willows had been the favorite resort of many a happy party through the years, but perhaps none were happier than Mattie Homer's circle that August. They picked blueberries in the morning on the bluffs beyond the beach and waded in the shallows in the afternoon. The sky was pearly through a good part of the day, but the haze was rising, not lowering, and it would be clear, everybody said, by evening. There was talk of fire balloons.

All during the drive from Townsend, Aurelia had wondered how she would feel when she saw the sea again. In the last year, she had thought more (and remembered more) about the wreck of the *Aspiration* than she had when she was in Boston. She wondered if she would be afraid, horrified of the breakers, or of storms coming in off the ocean. Sometimes she felt as though the sea must always be her enemy, and she was bound to hate it on sight.

"But the sea in my mind is not the real sea." She tried to

explain her contemplations to Mr. Winslow as they sat together on the sand, on her quilt of blue-green and black and zinnia red. "The real sea is so much more immense, it is just . . . *bigger* than any feelings I can have about it."

"When one looks at the sea," Mr. Winslow said, "all human feelings are minuscule. The sea washes them away for a while. Leaves one surprisingly peaceful, eh?"

He waved to his mother and father as they strolled along the strand, arm in arm.

The Homers had insisted that since Aurelia's uncle Joseph was going to be their guest, Aurelia must also come along. Mrs. Ellicott had first approved the plan, then announced that she and her children could also do with some sea air. (Amity had decided, though, to stay home and practice cooking and housekeeping for her father, who had to keep the mill open while his workers took their holidays. Laurence would be leaving for college soon, but he came to dinner more than once during the month, and lost a fair number of checker games to Mr. Ellicott, for a young man who was class salutatorian.)

Union had been torn between going to the shore and waiting for delivery of his Bayliss-Thomas, which Mr. Ellicott had ordered in advance of his son's rapidly approaching birthday. Amity, however, had reminded Union that a watched kettle never makes the express wagon come sooner, and Mr. Winslow and Mr. Charles promised to take him out in a catboat and teach him to sail. That idea trumped even the beloved bicycle for a while.

Most of the party had come by train, but, as the carriage would be needed, Mr. Peabodeau (Flanagan) drove it up, with Wayland's assistance. Mr. Hubbard had been in touch with the bank in St. Louis, and Julian Moylan's night of cards proved to have been fortunate, indeed. The gold alone was worth thousands, but in the years since the war, the silver miners had hit the mother lode. Overnight, the Harrigans had become wealthy. Only ink dapples would be left on his hands by the time Wayland started at Harvard in September; and for now, he thought he'd enjoy catboat lessons, himself.

Then, too, Miss Calantha — whom Uncle Joseph called "Miss Callie" and soon had everyone else doing likewise — had declared that, with Aurelia and Wayland both away, things would be so slow at the library, she might as well ask Mr. Flagg to take charge for a few weeks, so that she could go along with Aurelia and her uncle in the carriage, which was to go by way of Gloucester. Aurelia wished to pay a visit to the librarian, Mr. Sanborn, and shake his hand, and thank him and to see if he still had the quilt Grandmother Grunreiter had made by hand for Aurelia when she was born.

It was a great comfort to Miss Callie to reminisce with Jerry Harrigan and Joseph Grunreiter about her lost fiancé, and it gave her the greatest pleasure to watch Aurelia getting reacquainted with her beloved uncle. Joseph Grunreiter was an intelligent, practical man, for all his artistic sensitivity, and it was a simple thing for Miss Callie to take to her heart this friend who had come so far to ease her sorrow.

Elima had come to see them off. She had brought Aurelia a tin of chocolate biscuits and a ridiculous little oilcloth slicker for Uncle Adams, who was also going on holiday (to Amity's relief, Mr. Ellicott was to deal with Cicero until Union's return).

"Ma says, don't you worry about your locket," Elima explained. "Judge Twitchell heard that your uncle Joseph had gotten as far as asking Mr. Sinclair about you by name, all the way back last year. And that cad turned him from the door!"

Aurelia had felt the chill run right up her back and into her hair when she'd first heard that.

"I was probably right upstairs when it happened, or in the kitchen with Mrs. Prentice!" she exclaimed.

"He told me," Uncle Joseph had said, his gentle voice suffused with wrath, "that you had died of typhoid fever shortly after the Family Aid sent you to them. Then he excused himself, saying he was expected at his tailor's."

"And then started telling Mrs. Prentice she ought to retire," Aurelia had realized.

"Judge Twitchell said it sounded like a case of kidnapping and involuntary servitude. He promised he will point that out to Mr. Sinclair and tell him not to darken your doorway again, if he does not want the matter pursued — and to hand over your locket," Elima relayed with relish.

"Please tell your mother I am grateful," Aurelia said. "And as for this storm gear for Uncle Adams — I think it's the funniest thing I've ever seen, and I can hardly wait to hear what Mr. Winslow's father says about it!"

"But it will keep the little creature dry, too," Elima insisted agreeably. "I shall miss you while you are away, Aurelia. Is it true what Amity says? You and your uncle are to rent the upper floor of Miss Callie's and board with her? I call that dashing!"

"Yes, and I think it will be fun."

"Livia is already making snide remarks about how Bohemian an arrangement it appears to be."

"Oh, let her. Maybe we don't mind what other people think, as long as we know we are perfectly proper. This is where I have found friends I want to stay close to, and Uncle Joe wishes not to cause me any more loss. He has a good income, and I no longer need to work for my living. I may even be able to go to the new women's college at Harvard, when I'm ready. We are pursuing happiness. It is a patriotic thing to do."

Aurelia pried the top off the biscuit tin, and they each took one and nibbled contentedly.

"Do you have a middle name, Elima?" she asked after a

moment of chocolate. "I think I shall keep Sandborn for a middle name. It is really part of me, after all these years."

"Elima *is* my middle name. I'm called by it, not to be confused with Ma."

"Do you mean to tell me that you are Bonny Elima Worthy, all this time?" Aurelia demanded. "My goodness, I think I shall call you Bonny, if your mother prefers Beulah anyway. You are much more a Bonny, I think."

One thing that Aurelia liked about Miss Worthy was that her face was an open book. At that moment, the story writ there was a happy one.

And so, they gathered at the edge of the sea. Mrs. Prentice would be arriving with Mrs. Sinclair at the end of the week, for Jonathan and Kate had come to the Willows for their honeymoon and had loved it ever since. And Uncle Joseph had broken wonderful news to Aurelia, reminding her that he'd already been planning to come to Maine.

"Petit Manan is just up the coast from here. There was something I did not trust about Mr. E. Hancock Sinclair, and I wanted to start from scratch again, looking for you. I was going to go up to the Shankses' place and talk to Annabelle's mother. Your *grandmère* is still alive and healthy, *meine Aura Lee*. We are going to take a carriage ride up to visit her. And your cousins — the ones on this side of the family . . . your aunt Camille — your mother's sister — and her husband."

A family! Aurelia thought. *My* family. *Ours.*

There was to be a clambake on the beach that evening, and Mrs. Mattie had promised a special event. Mr. Winslow had decided his new painting was complete. The first thing he had done upon arriving at the Willows was to set up a mosquito net like a tent in his room, and put a final coat of varnish over the paint. By late afternoon, the varnish would be dry. His younger brother, Arthur, and Arthur's wife, Alice, would come over to the inn from their summer cottage farther down the beach, and Mr. Winslow would bring the painting out on the long veranda of the inn for everyone to have a look.

"Did you hear the rumor Union wheedled out of the innkeeper?" Wayland asked Aurelia as they sat, barefoot, among the tumbled boulders where a little rivulet of freshwater ran down to disappear in the surf.

"I don't think I need to, if it is another story about whale blubber in the fried onions, or Captain Kidd's treasure under the pilings of the pier," she replied with a laugh.

"No, I think this one has something to it. It would seem that Miss Louisa Alcott will be staying here next week. They say she is setting her new novel here."

"My word!" Aurelia exclaimed. "Why, Mrs. Prentice will introduce us, I am sure. They are old friends. You see, you *will* meet Mr. Emerson! Your career as a scholar is opening before you like a captain's spyglass." Despite the contentment of the moment, Aurelia noticed she was beginning to dread how soon Wayland would be off to Harvard.

"I have started writing poems again," Wayland admitted.

After a moment, Aurelia broke the silence that had suddenly arisen between them. (The truth was, she'd had an impulse to kiss him, but there were people all around.)

"I hope you will show some of them to me," was what she said.

"By and by," he answered. Then, "Well, you can read this bit later. It's not the grandest poetry, but I shan't apologize for it, for it's my own." He grinned. "You could say, I'm giving you my words." He took a bit of paper, folded many times, from his pocket, and handed it to her, but stopped her from opening it just yet. She could see that he had begun to sunburn, and she handed him the straw boater he had left hanging on a branch of driftwood. Then she watched regretfully as he covered his sunlit, newly trimmed hair.

She was holding her new parasol, but they would have had to be sitting very close to each other for it to shade them both, and that would probably not be proper. Would it? She thought she would ask Mrs. Ellicott — Mrs. Prentice would not be in for days, yet, and the weather promised sunshine.

When they walked back to the Willows, Union and Mr. Winslow had gathered a huge heap of seaweed for the fire pits, and now, with Mr. Winslow's mother's assistance, they were carefully pasting together tissue paper balloons to send aloft with burning candle stubs in them, once it got dark. Wayland strolled over to see how they were constructing the inner frames.

Mrs. Mattie had set up a folding Japanese screen on the veranda, and she was just coming out, leading one of the inn's waiters with a great silver salver bearing lemonade and frosted glasses.

Aurelia unfolded the paper Wayland had given her. It said,

> *Laurel crowned the hill*
> > *Like laurels on a brow,*
> *Exceeding expectations,*
> > *Though none could then see how.*

> *Exceeding expectations,*
> > *Yet more is promised, still:*
> *Cupped blossom constellations*
> > *The heavens' spring may fill.*

> *We raise our cups to Victory,*
> > *To Liberty and Knowledge.*
> *I raise my cup to Aurelia.*
> > *I'll write to you from college.*

Mrs. Mattie tapped a glass with a silver spoon so it rang like a delicate dinner bell.

"Come, everybody, gather around!" she called them all in from their conversations and games. "Winslow has completed his newest oil painting, and we are the first who are privileged to see it!"

When everyone had encircled the Japanese screen, Mr. Charles and Mr. Arthur lifted it and carried it away. Wayland reached for Aurelia's hand, and held it, while everyone gazed at *Girl and Laurel.*

She is not an Old World shepherdess, Mary with her lamb. She is not Aurelia Sandborn Grunreiter from Philadelphia. But the artist has seen her as a Pilgrim and a Yankee — perhaps a farm girl, perhaps a Nantucket Quaker, with her wood-based light basket: a young woman entirely American. She is the same color as the clouds and the sky, the same as the stones and the mountain laurel blossom, the same color as the deepest shadows.

The basket is pale yellow as sunlight, except for a touch of red.

Author's Note

⁂

Winslow Homer's long painting career exemplifies the independence, vigor, and originality of perhaps the most purely Yankee spirit in the art of the late nineteenth and early twentieth centuries. Born February 24, 1836, in Boston, Massachusetts, Win Homer lived, before the summer of 1879, the life story portrayed in *Of Flowers and Shadows* — up to a point. This book is a novel, and I have made up some characters and situations, and interpreted the historically documented events of a pivotal season in Homer's life, to suggest the subject matter and meaning of his art as a whole — both the work he did leading up to the oil painting *Girl and Laurel* upon which this book is based, and the changes in style and content he took up from 1879 onward until his death in 1910.

If you look through a collection of Homer reproductions, you will recognize the particular drawings and paintings that inspired many episodes of the story. *The Wreck of the Iron Crown*, for example, shows a three-masted bark, which suggested to me the fictional *Aspiration*. Sketches from his war notebooks portray cavalry officers — one, incidentally, very nearly lopping off a lightly scribbled cartoon head with a suspiciously Homeresque mustache. *The New Novel* shows the mysterious schoolteacher — but her gown is decidedly orange. (Perhaps I made up the notion that the watercolor has faded from the "touch of red" my fictionalized Homer devotes more words to than the real, shy, gruff Winslow probably would have, talking about what, to his eye, was evident.)

Homer was unique among American painters during those years in not choosing to study in Europe (he did live in England for a time), and in taking only a frugal minimum of art classes — just enough to learn how to use oil paints. His mother had taught him watercolors, and his first job had taught him etching skills — as well as the conviction that he preferred to work freelance forever rather than under any other person's employ. He kept this resolution from his twenty-first birthday onward, through years of magazine publication, mixed reviews, and low prices for such paintings as he was able to sell. He drew and painted steadily, year in and year out, while the critics' taste caught up with his radically new take on color, his populist vision of the ideal balance of humans and nature, his exquisite landscapes and seascapes and portraits of working people at their labor — and the critics grew steadily more respectful and enthusiastic. Today, many artists who were in vogue in Homer's era have lost their relevance, or seem quaint, sentimental, or imitators of the famous European painters. His work, though, continues to look fresh and lively, to engage our love of nature and our curiosity about humans coexisting among the elements.

Winslow Homer first came into the public eye as a special war correspondent illustrator during the Civil War. After the war, he lived for a few years in Washington Square in New York City, then back in Massachusetts, in Gloucester. He went camping and fishing in the Adirondacks, Canada, and around the Caribbean. His real family was as described here, including the temperaments I have ascribed to them.

The actual model for the oil painting *Girl and Laurel*, now at the Detroit Institute of Arts, was Fannie Sanders, whose family lived across the street from Mattie and Charles Homer. Fannie's father did own a sawmill, located as I have described my fictional Aurelia's employer's mill, up the road from the Homers' house and the sixteen-sided house I've claimed for Miss Calantha. Winslow painted Fannie the summer she was fourteen, after he abruptly broke off plans to vacation in Upper New York State.

Homer was a discreet Victorian gentleman, and he never discussed his love life, if any, for interviewers, or even left personal letters or journals alluding to such matters. His sister-in-law was quoted as once having told the story I repeat here, about the schoolteacher who chose a wealthy man over a struggling genius artist. Win Homer never married, and from

1879 onward, he gradually gave up painting women — the last few being fishermen's wives and daughters. For by this time, Winslow Homer had followed his inner artistic compass toward the work that would evoke his greatest powers to move and awe his viewer — paintings of the sea. Homer ultimately moved to Prout's Neck, Maine, to his family's seafront property. "The Sun will not rise, or set, without my notice, and thanks," is how he described his circumstances. He spent the rest of his life in a plain studio above the rocky shore, leaving during the winter for tropical climates and — surely not incidentally — the racially mixed society and music he had learned to enjoy in the war years, which New England, even in that exciting era of immigration, still did not provide.

The descriptions of Massachusetts life in this book are as realistic and historical as I could write. Louisa May Alcott and Ralph Waldo Emerson were not only stars of the intellectual world, they were popular celebrities of their time. Louisa's books were read by adults as well as young folk. Boston, especially, was a hotbed of literary clubs and readings, classes, and private charitable societies (the particular groups I name are made up). It also had its impoverished, disease-ridden tenements and people with harsh anti-Irish prejudice. Apart from town poor farms, the government didn't assure basic social welfare. Children were not protected by labor laws: The life of an orphan, widow, or domestic servant could be perilous.

Besides the Homers, the real Townsendites mentioned in

this story are Miletus Gleason; Mr. Howe; Mr. Nobby Flagg (in whose store the library really was housed for a time); Congressman Adams; the Knights; Thomas Roebuck; and Alphonse Peabodeau, to whom the Homer brothers always referred as Mike Flanagan. (I made up the details of that story and moved these people about somewhat in time — they are real historical figures, though I have made up their personalities in this book, to serve the story.) Most of the other characters' names I composed from local family and given names mentioned in Ithamar Sawtelle's *History of Townsend, Massachusetts*. Aurelia, Wayland and his family, Joseph Grunreiter, the Ellicotts, Miss Calantha, the Worthys, Mrs. Prentice, Captain Shank, Livia, the other students, and the Sinclairs are made-up characters, but Grunreiter's war career describes real campaigns. Uncle Adams is based on my own dog, Simon. There really was a resort called the Willows, as I have described it; Louisa Alcott was a guest and wrote about it in her novel *Jack and Jill*. Winslow Homer's brother, Arthur, and his wife honeymooned there. The Homers did donate generously to the public library (the séance table, as well as a branch reading room) and did give all the town children quarters for firecrackers. Mattie Homer really was one of the first women in town to ride a bicycle and to wear bloomers. Win did play the banjo.

In writing this book, I had the help and support of many people. In particular, I would like to thank my research guide,

Lee McTighe; Bob Hickcox and Edwin and Mary West of the Townsend Historical Society; the George Walter Vincent Smith Art Museum in Springfield, Massachusetts; my agent, Virginia Knowlton; Jean Feiwel and Aimee Friedman, my editors; my friends Eleanor Cook, Janet Sadler, and Sarah Hafner, who read early drafts; the ladies of my writers group — Corinne Demas, Barbara Diamond Goldin, Patty Maclachlan, Leslea Newman, Ann Warren Turner, and Jane Yolen — and the members of my kids' and teenagers' writing workshops, who have helpfully listened to and discussed sections of the work in progress. My family, and the rest of you who helped in more or less literary ways — you know who you are — Thank you!

—A. K.

ANNA KIRWAN is the author of nine books, including two novels in the bestselling Royal Diaries series, *Victoria: May Blossom of Britannia* and *Lady of Palenque, Flower of Bacal*. She lives in Massachusetts.

It's your turn to write a Portraits story!

$\mathcal{E}$nter the Portraits writing contest—and turn this portrait into a story! Who is the girl in this painting? Where does she live? What is her life like? It's all up to you! In **1500 words or less**, write your very own story about the girl in this portrait. The winning entry will be published in a future Portraits novel.

Enter by December 31, 2005

Send entries to: **Portraits Writing Contest**
557 Broadway
P.O. Box 715
NY, NY 10012

◾ **SCHOLASTIC**